“I didn’t mean t[illegible] work time, Lauren.”

This time there was no mistaking how her heart leapt when Garrett said her name. What was up with that? It’s not as though she was interested or anything.

“I’m glad you stopped by. I need to head back anyway. Can you recommend a good restaurant for lunch?”

His eyes brightened. “Want to have lunch with me?”

“Sure, that would be great,” she said, meaning it.

“Good,” he answered. “I’m really glad you came, Lauren.”

There was that heart flip again. He’d better quit saying her name or she’d need a pacemaker.

DIANN WALKER

and her husband, Jim, started on a three-mile trek through Amish country in 1997, and at that moment, she had no idea she was taking her first steps toward a new career. Inspired by their walk, she wrote an article, which was published a year later. Other articles soon followed. After studying fiction writing, she celebrated her first novella sale in 2001, with CBA bestselling novellas and novels, written as Diann Hunt, reaching the bookshelves soon afterward. Wanting to be used by God in the ministry of writing, Diann left her job as a court reporter in the fall of 2003 and now devotes her time to writing. Well, writing and spoiling her four granddaughters. She has been happily married forever and loves her family, chocolate, her friends, chocolate, her dog and, well, chocolate. Be sure to check out her Web site at www.diannhunt.com. Sign her guestbook and drop her an e-mail. And, hey, if you have any chocolate. . .

A MATCH MADE IN BLISS

DIANN WALKER

Published by Steeple Hill Books™

STEEPLE HILL BOOKS

ISBN 0-373-87357-3

A MATCH MADE IN BLISS

This edition published by arrangement with Steeple Hill Books.

www.SteepleHill.com

Printed in U.S.A.

Trust in the Lord with all your heart and
lean not on your own understanding; in all
your ways acknowledge Him, and
He will make your paths straight.

—*Proverbs* 3:5–6

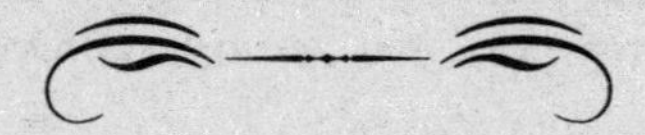

With heartfelt thanks:

To my wonderful agent, Karen Solem, for your constant support and wise counsel.

To my editor, Krista Stroever, for your upbeat attitude that always encourages me, and for your expertise that challenges me to grow as a writer. It is my privilege to work with you.

To my friend and kindred spirit, Colleen Coble, who patiently sees me through every crisis and critiques my words in their roughest form. I thank God for you.

To my supportive husband, without whom my stories would never have felt the warm embrace of a book binding. I love you more than words can say.

Most of all, to you, my readers, who are kind enough to spend a few hours of your time to journey through these pages with me.

May God bless you all.

Chapter One

"I can't believe you did this without even consulting me!" Garrett Cantrell stomped across the den of the Woods Inn Bed and Breakfast. His footsteps were muffled once he stepped on the oriental rug, then thumped again when he turned and walked across the hardwood floor.

He stopped and frowned at his daughters, who sat quietly on the sofa. "What were you thinking?" He turned to his firstborn. "Macy, you're a high school graduate—and older than most at that," Garrett said, referring to the childhood illness that had caused Macy to start school later than others, giving her almost a two-year edge over her peers. "You're old enough to know better. Would you appreciate it if I manipulated *your* life?"

Macy lifted her chin in a rebellious attitude. He shot her a quelling look, and she lowered it once again.

"And you." He looked at Molly. "You'll be a senior next year. How about I set you up with Reggie Snodgrass?" The look on her face would have been comical had Garrett not been in such a foul mood.

Reggie didn't exactly turn the girls' heads. Well, he did, but usually in the opposite direction. Everyone in the area knew Reggie had been sweet on Molly since first grade. He was tall, skinny, wore black-rimmed glasses, talked with a nasal twang and snorted every time he laughed. The typical high school geek.

Molly lifted her face to her dad, her eyes wide with fear. She wisely kept her mouth shut.

Garrett paced some more. "I knew I should have gotten rid of that computer." Stopping in front of them again, he said, "Let me get this straight. Because of your fascination with that reality TV stuff, you came up with the brilliant idea to advertise in a chat room, a contest called 'Win Daddy's Heart'? Then you left details on a message board."

The girls sat rooted like potted plants.

"You picked five applicants from pictures and bios e-mailed to you and offered the women a free two-week stay at our B and B."

Completely mute. Macy's right eye twitched.

"You figured we could live off our investments, so the two weeks without paying guests would be no big deal." Still pacing, he said this more to himself than to them. "Then you took it upon yourselves to write these contestants' names on the scheduling book so I wouldn't double book our rooms. When they come, their afternoons will be free, and I am to take them out individually on the nights of my choosing." He stopped and turned to them.

At this, Molly nodded ever so slightly.

"We all are to mill around and just get to know one another over the two weeks, and by the end of their stay, you're hoping someone will win my heart, is that it?"

Molly's face brightened for just a moment. She nodded enthusiastically as if her dad was finally catching on. Macy was much more cautious—and sensible. She didn't move. Not one inch. He couldn't even tell if she was breathing. Her eye continued to twitch.

He blew out a long sigh. "Let me see that." He pointed to the file in Molly's hands.

She handed it to him. "It's all right there, Dad. We checked out every applicant, making sure they were compatible with you." She smiled tentatively, as if proud of herself for being organized with the whole thing.

He glanced through the file. "There are only four applicants here."

Molly shifted uncomfortably on her seat and looked at Macy. "Well, uh, we seem to have misplaced the information on the fifth applicant," Molly admitted.

"She did call, though, and said she probably wouldn't be able to make it. Something came up. So I don't think we have anything to worry about," Macy added.

Garrett rolled his eyes. "Perfect." He slapped the file against the palm of his hand and pulled up a chair. Sitting down with a thump, he faced them. A slight pause followed. "Look," he said in a gentle voice, "I know you're trying to help me. I miss your mom, that's true, but that's not why I haven't dated. I just haven't met anyone I want to date."

"But Dad, Mom died three years ago. It's time."

Molly laid each word before him as if tiptoeing across a room.

"That's not for you to decide," Garrett snapped. His youngest daughter looked every inch the image of her mother. Her dark-brown hair lay softly across her shoulders like a silken scarf, and her brown eyes glistened in the morning light. He felt his insides go soft. A headache throbbed over his eyes, causing him to rub his forehead. "Okay, here's what you have to do. You write to each of these ladies and tell them there's been a big mistake. The search for someone for your dad is off. No free vacations for the applicants. The game's over." He started to stand.

"We can't," Molly offered in a weak voice.

He stopped in midair, turned to her and sat back down. A sick feeling washed over him. A feeling that said this wasn't going to go away. "Why not, Molly?"

She cleared her throat and stared at the toes of her sneakers. "Um, because a couple of ladies will be coming tonight. The others will be in tomorrow."

He gaped at them in disbelief. The grandfather clock ticked from the opposite wall, punctuating the scant moments of freedom remaining. "You've heard the story of Jacob and Esau? You know, the selling of the birthright and all?"

His daughters watched him, saying nothing.

"Well, just know your positions in this family are hanging by a thread." He paced again. "If we send them home, it could be bad publicity for the place." He mumbled the words to himself. He continued to think it through. The women would have paid for their airfare—he couldn't exactly make them turn around and go home. He stopped in front of his daughters. "I can't believe this." He looked at them incredulously. "I actually have to go through with this."

Right then the front door creaked open. "Yoo-hoo, anybody home? Hello?" A singsong voice echoed through the entryway. "Anyone here? Yoo-hoo?"

Garrett cringed. His eyes narrowed and he pinned his daughters with a stern glare.

They gulped in unison.

Between clenched teeth he hissed, "If you weren't so old, I'd put you both up for adoption." With that he turned and stomped out of the room.

Chapter Two

"Oh, come on, Lauren, you have to go," Candace and Gwen chimed in over their conference call.

"You need to get away from this place. Get over Jeff, think about where you want to work next and just plain rest," Candace encouraged.

"But tomorrow? I don't have anything packed."

"You always pack light anyway, Lauren," Candace encouraged.

Lauren Romey released a slight smile in spite of the anxiety welling up inside. Candace Windsor and Gwen Sandler had been two of Lauren's best friends since college days. If anyone could talk her into anything, they could. Though Candace lived in Nevada, Gwen lived in Arizona and Lauren lived in Indiana, the three managed to meet every year in Candace's childhood hometown of Bliss Village, California, just a little way from beautiful Lake Tahoe. Lauren had fallen in love with the scenic town the first time she'd gone there, so the idea of going back ahead of their yearly meeting—

even for a suspicious surprise getaway like the one her friends were now offering—held a certain amount of charm.

"Now, I can hear your mind clicking from here," Candace was saying. "Don't worry about the money. It is our gift to you, and it would be rude of you to refuse us."

Oh, sure, they always played on her weakness of wanting to please others.

"And since you haven't found another job yet—"

Lauren winced. "Don't remind me."

"You're free as a bird," Gwen added. "I'm sorry, I'm not trying to make you feel bad, but it's a perfect time for you to get away, before you're tied up with new employment."

Unfortunately, the new employment thing didn't seem to be a problem. Despite the number of resumés the unemployed corporate attorney had sent out, she didn't exactly have employers beating down her door to get to her. The fact that she was "let go" from her prior job, she was sure didn't help matters.

"Besides that, we have a surprise," Gwen said in her usual perky voice. A voice that sometimes irritated Lauren.

"Gwen, don't give everything away," Candace warned.

Uh-oh, these two were up to something. "Do you need to tell me something?"

"Uh, no, you'll find out soon enough. Let's just say we've taken care of everything and all you have to do is show up."

"That's what I'm afraid of," Lauren pointed out.

"What's that?" Candace asked.

"The 'we've taken care of everything' part."

Gwen laughed. "You worry too much, Lauren. Just go and have fun." To Gwen, life was just one big party.

Oh, well, there was no use fighting them. Besides, Lauren needed to get out of town. Away from Jeff and Camilla. Away from the memories.

"Now, write this down," Candace was saying. "Woodwards' Bed and Breakfast." She proceeded to give Lauren the address and phone number. "Your flight leaves at seven-ten tomorrow morning. One short layover and transfer."

Lauren groaned.

"Sorry, that's the best we could do. Grab a taxi and you'll be there by early evening."

"What about Nocchi?" Lauren asked, referring to her shih tzu.

"They said you could bring her." Gwen laughed. "We checked."

It seemed they had thought of everything.

Lauren was silent.

"You still there?" Candace wanted to know.

"Yes."

"Are we all set?"

Lauren hesitated, then offered a resigned "Yes."

"Whoo-hoo," Gwen called from the line.

"Great!" Candace chimed in. "I'm going to London with Mom and Dad for a week. Should get back to the States during your second week. I'll call you then."

"Okay," Lauren said, feeling none too sure about this whole thing.

"Bon voyage," Gwen called with a laugh.

"She's not going on a cruise," Candace said dryly.

Showing her good-natured spirit, Gwen simply said, "Oh, yeah. Well, adios."

Candace groaned. Being the more sensible one of the two, she too sometimes struggled with Gwen's constant bubbling. "Have a wonderful time, Lauren. Who knows, this trip could possibly change your life."

I could use a changed life, she wanted to say. "Thanks, Candace. Thanks, Gwen. You two are the best."

After they all exchanged goodbyes, Lauren put the phone down and stared at it. Candace's words rang in her ears. *This trip could possibly change your life.* Lauren wanted to believe that. Her life couldn't get any worse.

She looked around her bedroom decorated with modern furnishings and deep crimson-colored walls with white trim. How long had she lived in this apartment? Three years now? As a two-bedroom, it wasn't huge, but it was spacious enough for her. She liked the layout of the place and the fact that it was brand new when she moved in. With it being situated so close to work was a definite plus. She wasn't sure what had held her back from buying a home, but given the current situation of living off her savings, she was glad she wasn't tied to a mortgage. Besides, with her best friends living in other states, the bigger home would only increase her feelings of loneliness.

Lauren left her bedroom and headed toward the attic to retrieve her luggage, all the while praying her friend was right.

By Saturday afternoon four of the contestants had arrived. No one was sure if number five would show.

Since they had lost her application, Macy and Molly seemed a little relieved.

After dinner, Garrett stepped outside behind their B and B. Twilight had just settled over Bliss Village, and he needed a breath of fresh air. Macy and Molly could take care of entertaining the guests for now.

Once outside, Garrett gazed at the evening sky. Was he crazy for trying to run this place? After all, the B and B had been his wife's dream, not his. They'd only lived there, what, two years when she died? Hardly seemed possible that he and the girls had lived there five years already.

He walked over to get Bear, his black Lab, from his pen. He had never seen such a diverse group of women. Where in the world had his daughters found them—on weirdbadandugly.com? He sighed. Okay, he wasn't being fair. They weren't ugly, after all. But they were, well, a little weird. He kicked a rock out of his path. Maybe they weren't strange at all. It might just be him—he didn't know what to look for in a woman anymore.

Bear trotted alongside him as they took a pine-laden path in the woods behind his B and B.

Besides, Garrett had to admit Gracie appealed to him, with her lithe body, long brown hair that looked soft enough to wallow his face in and brown eyes that could match that of any doe in the county. It had been some time since he'd been attracted to a woman.

If only he could duct-tape her mouth.

There was something about her voice, or maybe it was the way she said things, or what she said. He didn't know. But he had a sneaking suspicion if he was with her for very long, they'd have to put him in a strait-jacket. In fact, he figured the government could use her as an instrument of torture in times of war.

No wonder she lived on a mountain.

Maybe he should reserve judgment. Perhaps she was nervous. He'd give her the benefit of the doubt.

He'd try to give them *all* the benefit of the doubt.

Garrett came to the wicker bench he had placed on the rough trail and sat down. The air smelled damp and heavy with the scent of pine. This place calmed him like nothing else could. Birdsong whispered through the trees that cooled and protected him when he visited during the heat of the day.

Bear walked around, sniffed here and there, then strutted back. With the stance of a lawn ornament he sat at attention beside Garrett's feet.

Brown cones and pine needles littered the area. Garrett sighed and ran a hand through his thick dark hair. He couldn't remember such a stressful day. Oh, he knew his daughters meant well, they constantly nagged him about dating, but he had a feeling the next two weeks would be about as comfortable as wearing a suit and tie on a fishing boat. He leaned over and scratched Bear's head. The dog leaned in for a good rub.

"What am I going to do, Bear?" Garrett kept scratching. "There's not a woman there I can relate to. I know the girls have put a lot of work into this, so I have to follow through, but it won't be easy. I have a feeling we'll be making lots of trips out here, ol' boy." Bear looked up and Garrett was almost certain he saw a smirk on the hound's face. Sometimes Garrett felt his dog was close to human.

He rubbed his forehead. Why did Susie have to leave him? He wouldn't be going through this whole mess if she were still here. They had so many dreams for their future. He could still remember how her eyes used to sparkle whenever she talked about the B and B. She had such a passion for people, for…life. He sighed. Those days were over and there was nothing he could do about it now. But, oh, how he missed her.

How long he sat there Garrett wasn't sure, but darkness had fallen over the trees, with only slivers of moonlight poking through the branches. When he stepped into the clearing, the full moon sailed high in the sky and lit his way back to the house. He hoped to sneak up to his room, since the actual "contest" didn't start until tomorrow. With any luck, they'd all disappear with the morning fog.

Garrett and Bear trudged the path toward the house. "Good night, ol' boy," Garrett said, hooking the hound to a chain and giving him one more scratch behind the ears. Then Garrett straightened. As if on cue, Bear yawned and walked back to his doghouse, completing their nightly ritual.

When Garrett stepped inside the back door and into the kitchen, he was pleasantly surprised by the silence that met him. Seeing a note on the kitchen island, he walked over and picked it up. "Dad, we took the women to the coffee shop. Figured you'd appreciate some time to prepare for tomorrow. Be back in a little while. Love, Molly."

"Ah, thanks, girls," he said to the empty house, feeling himself relax. Pulling a cold soft drink from the fridge, he grabbed a hunting magazine and settled into an overstuffed beige chair in the den.

This evening held promise after all.

Recognizing some of the familiar sights in Bliss Village, Lauren knew the taxi had to be getting close to the bed-and-breakfast, though not close enough for her. The stench of stale smoke and cheap cologne filled the car, making her wish she'd not eaten the greasy hamburger at the airport. Even Nocchi whined and pawed at her nose. A country-and-western tune whined through the radio speakers, while the taxi driver concentrated more on scratching the whiskers on his face than driving.

Frustration mounted as Lauren fumbled through her bags in search of—but not finding—the paper with the information on where she would be staying. The bed-and-breakfast was located on Pine Road in Bliss Village and the name had "wood" in it—she remembered that much. If the driver went to Pine Road, they were sure to find it. She finally gave up her search for the paper, shoved everything back inside her bag and zipped it closed.

She glanced out her window. Earlier, they had passed a few quaint, cozy Victorian homes with warm, inviting lampposts and porches. Now they approached a more rustic area lined with cabins and woodsy-type homes. Lauren saw a sign on the lawn of the next property. Woods Inn Bed and Breakfast.

"There it is!" she said, pointing.

The driver hit the brakes and screeched to a sudden halt at the curb, practically giving Lauren a whiplash in the process. She knew some personal-injury attorneys who would love this guy.

Quickly she checked on her dog in the carrier beside her feet on the floor. The driver got out of the car and Lauren followed suit, then reached back inside for the carrier. Once outside, she took in a big breath of fresh air. The driver slid her bag from the trunk as if he hadn't the strength to lift it, and let it drop on the street with a thunk. Feeling less than charitable, she paid him reluctantly for his services.

The taxi squealed off and she glanced around the property dense with pines and large, leafy green foliage. Gothic arches adorned the thick massive stone structure that loomed before her. Not exactly the cozy Victorian she had expected, but it had a sort of earthy quality about it.

Lauren grabbed her things and looked at the front door. "Well, here goes nothing." Trudging up the incline toward her home for the next two weeks, she hoped Candace and Gwen were right and that she could get some rest here.

Once she reached the door, she set her luggage down beside her, took a deep breath and knocked.

Upon hearing the doorbell, Garrett leaned his head back against the comfy chair and glanced toward the ceiling. "Great, contestant number five." He squeezed his eyes shut for a fraction of a second, as if it would all go away like a bad dream. With reluctance he pulled himself from the deep chair, walked down the hall, around to the front door and opened it. The visitor took him by surprise.

"Hi, I'm Lauren Romey. I have a reservation here."

Now here was a welcome sight. Dressed in stylish jeans and a long white T-shirt adorned with a classy silver belt at her waist, this woman had definite potential. It didn't hurt that she had hair the color of buttercups and eyes that made him feel he had stepped into the clear, blue-green water of Emerald Bay. His spirits improved considerably.

"Garrett Cantrell, owner of the place." He shook her hand, then stepped aside to allow her entrance. "So you decided to come after all, huh?"

She raised her eyebrows and looked at him with surprise. "Oh, uh, yeah."

"Here, let me get that for you." He reached for her luggage. In her other hand, he noted a dog in a carrier.

"You have a dog, Miss Romey?"

"That's what they call 'em where I come from."

"Oh, a guest with a sense of humor," he said with a smirk.

"Is that a problem?"

"The humor or the dog?"

She laughed with a little hesitation. Seeming to sense they were talking about her, Nocchi whined and pawed at the floor of her carrier. "Shh," Lauren scolded. She turned back to Garrett. "They told me I could bring her. I assure you, Nocchi is harmless."

"Nocchi?"

"Yes, spelled N-o-c-c-h-i, but it's pronounced no-key."

He thought he'd eaten an Italian dinner once by that name.

"Her name is actually Pinocchio. I call her Nocchi for short."

Now he'd heard everything. A tiny black dog with a

barely visible nose named Pinocchio. Okay, that was weird. Weirdbadandugly.com. Garrett stuck his face closer to the carrier to get a look at the animal. He rubbed his eyes and peered in again. The dog was actually wearing a dress. Not only that, but a denim sailor-type cap festooned with a matching bow sat a little crookedly on her head. Now he'd seen everything. Talk about your froufrou dogs. This was just wrong. No animal should have to suffer that type of humiliation. Garrett leaned in farther and squinted. "Is there something wrong with her, um, eyes?" he asked, pointing.

"Huh? Oh, that." With a defensive jerk, Lauren pulled the carrier away from him. "She's—" Lauren lifted her chin "—cross-eyed."

Certain he had misunderstood, Garrett leaned toward her. "She's what?"

Her chin rose another notch. "I said Nocchi is cross-eyed." Her expression dared him to challenge her.

He thought she was about to add, "You got a problem with that?" But she didn't. He bit the sides of his mouth to keep from laughing.

She turned back to her pooch. "Poor thing. She was dropped as a pup, and they said she's been that way ever since." Lauren stuck her fingers through the grated door of the carrier and stroked Nocchi. "I do have to be careful moving the furniture."

Garrett shuddered.

Lauren missed it; she continued to stroke her dog. "She's a shih tzu," Lauren explained. "She never makes any noise—" Nocchi suddenly yipped and jerked back, making Lauren almost drop the carrier.

"Oh, I'm sorry, Nocchi," Lauren cooed, checking the

dog over. She looked back to Garrett. "I think I poked her in the eye."

Garrett looked at Lauren's long, manicured nails. He wondered if the dog would ever see again.

Lauren hurried on. "She's housebroken and won't be a problem, I promise." The woman lifted those Emerald Bay eyes to him.

How did women do that? It seemed they had an internal button marked "charm weapon" that they turned on when they needed it. Garrett winced inside, but his lips rose at the corners. There was a strict "no pets" policy—why would Macy and Molly tell her a dog was all right? He sighed. He couldn't turn her away. She was the one normal applicant in the group. Well, at least she *appeared* normal. Still, the dog was questionable.

"That's fine, Miss Romey—"

"Please, call me Lauren." Her eyes twinkled.

Oh, sure, now that I've accepted her dog, it's Lauren. "Lauren," he repeated. "If you want to step into the front room, I have your key on a desk there."

As they walked down the hall, Garrett heard her footsteps behind him and wondered what she would think of the place. A woman like her no doubt stayed in only the nicest inns and hotels. He squared his shoulders. Why should he care what she thought? Woods Inn could rival the best of them.

She gasped as he led her into an enormous room with a massive stone fireplace that stretched to a cathedral ceiling. He glanced back at her and followed her gaze from the brown beams arched above to the dark warm carpet beneath their feet. Though the room was large, the subdued lighting that shone from corner lamps gave it a sort of cozy feel. Well, that was what his girls had told him, anyway.

"This is very nice," Lauren said as though she meant it.

"Thanks. My girls offer the feminine touch with the plants and fluffy pillows, all that. If I had my way, I'd have bear heads mounted on the wall."

Lauren grimaced.

Garrett laughed. "Yeah, that's kind of what my daughters thought."

"How old are your girls?"

"Macy is nineteen and Molly is sixteen," he said. "Macy had a childhood illness that caused her to start school late."

"Won't be long until you will have an empty nest—well, except for your visitors."

He thought a moment. "It's funny. My wife and I were working hard to make the adjustment easier—you know, dating, still making time for each other so that we wouldn't grow apart and then be strangers once the girls were gone. With my wife's death, I'm afraid the adjustment won't be quite as easy." He didn't like the vulnerable feeling that swept over him. Walking over to a large wooden desk, he made a couple of notes in the log book and handed Lauren a key. "Would you care for a snack before you settle in? It's on the house," he said with a smile.

"No, thank you. I'm pretty tired."

"Here, let me help you to your room," he said, grabbing her luggage.

In silence they climbed the small spiral staircase

together. Garrett opened the door to her room, allowed her entrance and placed the luggage just inside the door. She turned to him. "I will need to take Nocchi out. Is there a preferred area?"

He thought a moment. "You'd better let me know when you're ready. I have a black Lab outside." Alpha dog, he wanted to say. The thought made him feel proud, even a trifle studly. "Bear is chained, but I don't want him to startle Nocchi." One look at Bear, and she'd wish she'd left her dog at home.

"Thank you," she said before closing her door.

He turned to go back down the stairs, feeling a tad ashamed of his thoughts. What had gotten into him anyway? He was grumpy, that's what. He didn't appreciate the position in which his girls had placed him. Not one bit. As Garrett walked down the stairs, he wondered how on earth he could endure the next couple of weeks with five strange women and a cross-eyed hairball.

Chapter Three

A sense of restfulness greeted Lauren the moment she stepped into her room. The pleasing scent of cinnamon wafted from a dainty dish of potpourri. Compliments of Garrett's daughters, no doubt.

She wondered about these girls who had lost their mother. Her heart squeezed with compassion for them. She looked forward to meeting them. They had to be beautiful if they resembled Garrett in any way. Thick dark hair crowned his head with soft curls, stopping short of wide, dark eyes. She would not have been surprised to learn he had Greek ancestry. His manner seemed cautiously friendly, almost business-professional with a smidgen of warmth thrown in for good measure.

She didn't need to be thinking about the hotelier's good looks.

She lowered Nocchi's carrier on the floor and glanced around. Earth tones covered the bed, plump pillows and window tops. Color-coordinated pictures depicting woodsy scenes hung here and there against the pine-paneled walls. A heavy wooden rocker with thick cushions added the perfect touch to this rustic yet inviting bedroom. At one corner a door led to a good-sized bath area, complete with a roomy shower.

Lauren took a deep breath. She was glad she had come—this was exactly what she needed. Picking up her cell phone, she decided she'd call Gwen, since Candace had already left for London.

Punching the numbers, she waited while the phone rang.

"Hello?" Gwen answered with her usual enthusiasm.

"Hi, Gwen. This is Lauren. Just wanted to let you know I made it to the B and B and it is wonderful, just as you and Candace said."

"Oh, I'm so glad, Lauren!" Gwen said, her chewing gum snapping as she talked. "I think you're going to have a wonderful time." She popped a bubble. Lauren couldn't understand for the life of her why Gwen—a grown woman—still insisted on chewing bubble gum. To her credit, she did try to chew discreetly, but a bubble here and there always managed to pop during a conversation, giving her all the grace of a junior high school student. "I'm praying for you."

"Thank you." Despite her gum and party attitude, Gwen had a way of making those with whom she talked feel as though they were the most important people in the world. Lauren's heart warmed as the two discussed her trip to California and how much fun she was sure to have. "I don't know what I'd do without you and Candace."

Gwen's gum stopped snapping and she seemed to

grow pensive, something she didn't do often. "We have a special friendship. We're always here for you, just as you've been there for us. "Now," she said, her perky voice back in place, gum popping, "you get some rest while you're there, okay? No more doom and gloom!"

"Will do. And Gwen?"

"Yeah?"

"Thanks again."

"You're welcome."

Lauren put her cell phone on the nightstand and lifted her luggage onto the bed. Nocchi whined, obviously wanting out of her prison.

"Oh, dear, I forgot about you, didn't I?" Lauren walked over and opened the small door of the carrier. Scooping the eight-pound, black shih tzu into her arms, Lauren cuddled the dog, then scratched the white stripe that went from just under the dog's chin down to her belly. "I'd better take you outside before you get too comfortable." Nocchi snuggled her head into Lauren's neck, a gesture that brought them both sheer pleasure.

"Okay, let's go." Lauren adjusted Nocchi's hat, latched a leash onto her collar, walked her out of the room and down the stairs. She saw the owner bent over paperwork at his desk. Nocchi veered a little too far over and bumped into a stand. Garrett looked up.

"Sorry," Lauren said to Garrett while tugging at the leash to pull Nocchi to her. She rubbed Nocchi's noggin. "Is this a good time to take her out?"

"No problem." He stood and started toward the back door. "Come this way," he called over his shoulder.

Lauren followed him through the dining room, into the kitchen and out the back door, taking in his long strides, tall, lean frame, sweatshirt and jeans. Something about him made her want to put on a sweat suit, scrunch into a blanket and cuddle with someone under the stars. Jeff Levinger's face popped into view, causing an ache in her heart. Six months, and she still hurt as if they had broken up only yesterday. People don't just fall in and out of love—it takes time to get over the pain. She remembered her promise to herself to wait a year before starting another relationship. Not that there was a problem. She didn't exactly have men waiting in line to take her out.

"Why don't you hold on to Nocchi, and I'll keep Bear chained, but we can let them get to know each other a moment. Would that be all right?"

His voice chased away the ache in her heart—for now. "Well..." She bit her lip and thought a moment. "I suppose it would be all right." She followed him over to the doghouse, where a black Lab ambled out of the opening, his tail wagging. A good sign, she thought.

Nocchi started barking like crazy. Lauren and Garrett worked to calm their dogs.

Once Nocchi quieted, Lauren listened as the man soothed his dog. That spoke well of him. Men who were good to animals were true heroes in her book. This trip might be worthwhile after all.

"I think Bear's ready," Garrett said, motioning for Lauren to bring Nocchi over.

Carefully she stepped close to Bear and squatted down so the dogs could sniff one another while Nocchi stayed in her arms. Bear's tail continued to wag. Nocchi sniffed back, her tail wagging with a trace of caution.

"You want to put her down? I'll see that Bear behaves."

"If he doesn't, I'm afraid I'll have to hurt you," she said with only a hint of teasing before gently placing Nocchi inches from her on the ground.

Garrett studied her a moment. Almost as if he considered taking her on.

"I'm kidding."

"Good thing. I haven't worked out in a while."

"Oh, now who's the comedian?" she kidded before adding, "Like I could hurt you."

He straightened his back. Had she imagined it, or did she see him flex?

"Well, you could try," he said, quirking an eyebrow and flashing a biceps.

They both laughed. "Hey, it seems they're hitting it off," Lauren said, looking at the dogs. "Guess you're safe."

"Well, would you look at that?"

"You're surprised?"

"You have to admit they're very different. I've never seen Bear take to a little dog before. I knew he wouldn't hurt her, but I didn't expect him to actually like her." The two dogs appeared instant friends.

"Must be the clothes. I mean, an outfit can make all the difference," Lauren said while examining a slight chip in her red nail polish. "I looked a long time before I found a clothing site for dogs on the Internet that I could be happy with." She looked up to find Garrett gaping.

Garrett snapped his mouth closed. Men just didn't appreciate the finer things in life.

"She's a little self-conscious about the whole cross-eyed thing, so I thought some nice doggie clothes would make her feel better." Lauren smiled. "Isn't that right, Nocchi," she cooed, patting the dogs' head.

He stared at her a moment then lifted a weak smile.

They engaged in a friendly chat while they watched the dogs interact. Lauren told him she was a corporate attorney from Indiana. An ex-corporate attorney who had lost her job, she should have said, but why throw in the gory details? Besides, she was still a corporate attorney, just an unemployed one.

Garrett told about his wife's dream of owning a B and B, and he talked about his daughters. By the time they heard the car doors in the parking area, they had gleaned quite a bit of knowledge about each other.

Lauren took Nocchi for a little walk around the grounds, while Garrett went into the house to greet everyone. When Lauren stepped inside, she heard the chatter coming from the house and hoped it wouldn't be that noisy all the time. She really did need some peace and quiet. They were still standing around talking when she walked into view. The moment everyone saw her, all talk came to a complete stop.

Lauren scooped Nocchi into her arms, more for comfort than propriety, and looked up. "Hello." The odd mix of women looked none too friendly, from her point of view. Of course, she had to tell herself she was stressed and probably overreacting.

The wide grin on Garrett's face encouraged her. Everyone looked from him back to her. He walked to her side and gently grabbed her arm, a gesture everyone seemed to notice. "Ladies, I want you to meet Lauren Romey."

A cold chill seemed to sweep across the room like an arctic blast. No one in the room was smiling but Garrett. She didn't know what was going on, but there was a definite competitive feel in the air.

"Hello," she said.

Garrett gently guided Lauren around the room. "Lauren, this is Gracie Skinner." Lauren felt a trifle intimidated by the tall, thin beauty with perfect hair and teeth. This woman could model for any upscale New York agency. Lauren wondered why Gracie would be at the B and B, and decided she must need a break, too. "Gracie comes from Castle Mountain, Tennessee," Garrett said.

"My, my, what a funny little dog," Gracie said, pointing at Nocchi's hat.

Why couldn't anyone appreciate Nocchi's upscale appearance?

Gracie locked eyes with Lauren. "Howdy, Lucy."

"Um, it's Lauren," she corrected.

"Oh," Gracie said with a fake laugh, "ain't I bad?" She waved her hand and walked away.

Suddenly the woman didn't look so beautiful.

Garrett pulled Lauren to the next woman. "This is Ellen Little from Tangly, Ohio." Though she was a bit skinny, the woman's red hair had a shine that could rival a washed apple. She put a hand to her meager chest and took a deep breath. Behind her trendy glasses her eyes were an interesting green, almost the color of a budding leaf. After pushing her glasses back up her nose, for a fleeting second she lifted her eyes and upturned mouth. "Hello," she said in a near whisper, barely extending her hand. Maybe she was intimidated by Miss Model's presence, too.

Moving on down the line, Garrett said, "This is Billie Gibbons from Goosefield, Montana."

"Hello," Lauren said, thinking an attacker would be hard-pressed to take on this one. Still, the way the woman's brown hair curled around her eyes and face made her appear soft and reachable.

"How ya doing, kid?" Billie asked, pulling Lauren and Nocchi into a bear hug and giving Lauren a stiff pat on the back. She wondered if she ought to cough in response. Nocchi squirmed, no doubt to get some air.

"This is Nikki Spartan from San Francisco." This one scared Lauren. Her skin was as pale as bleached muslin, yet she seemed to have a thing for black—black spiked hair with blond tips, black lipstick and a black leather jacket and pants. Lauren felt as if she should be searching her pocket for pepper spray while she tried not to stare at the woman's silver nose ring.

The woman's lip curled in typical Elvis fashion. "Nice dog," she said with a grunt.

Okeydokey, Lauren thought, mentally rolling her eyes. She was ready to make a hasty retreat to her room.

"And these are my daughters," Garrett said with obvious pride, pointing to two strikingly beautiful teenagers. Their friendly faces made her instantly feel better.

"This is Macy, who will be leaving me and going off to college in the fall."

"Hello," Macy said.

Lauren beamed at the budding woman standing before her. Black ringlets started at her crown and spiraled down to her shoulders. Her fringed curls stopped short of her eyebrows, emphasizing her dark liquid eyes—eyes that appeared to hold a touch of sadness. "Hello, Macy. So nice to meet you."

"And this is the squirt—I mean Molly." He aimed a mischievous wink at Lauren.

"D-a-a-a-d!" his youngest daughter said, shoving him playfully on the arm.

"Nice to meet you, Molly."

"Hi." Looking every inch her sister only with straight hair landing midway down her back, Molly lifted a smile. "Glad you could make it."

Why did everyone think she wouldn't make it? Had Candace told them she might not come? "Thank you" was all Lauren said. Though each woman looked distinct in appearance, Lauren had to admit each one was attractive in her own way—even Goth Woman. As the women began to chitchat among themselves, Lauren made excuses to Garrett and his daughters and left for her room.

She trudged up the stairs. It seemed odd to her that there were only women guests. She thought that couples normally frequented these kinds of places, especially in a quaint town such as Bliss Village, fairly close to Lake Tahoe. Something told her there was more to this vacation than met the eye. Oh, well, she was there to please her friends and get some much-needed R&R. She would soon go home and search for another job. Another life.

Once inside her room, she removed Nocchi's hat and dress, then settled her on the floor. Lauren plopped onto the bed, falling back into the plump softness of the pillows, and tucked her hands behind her head. A restful two weeks awaited her. No more thoughts of court hearings, client contacts, billing logs, job hunts, or—most important—Jeff. Rest. Sweet rest.

A time of starting over.

Garrett's image popped into her mind, though she couldn't imagine why.

The morning sun blazed through Lauren's window, waking her. She glanced at the clock and couldn't believe she had slept until eleven o'clock on a Sunday. Back home she'd have already attended the worship service and be halfway through Sunday school by now.

Normally an early riser by nature, she figured she must have needed the sleep. She snuggled farther into her covers, relishing her moment of laziness. The bed held her like a comforting hug. That's how she used to feel in Jeff's arms.

Until he dumped her.

Lauren threw off the covers with a yank. "With my best friend!" She looked at Nocchi. "He broke our engagement to be with Camilla. Supposedly my best friend. Well, she had been my best friend all through school until college. How could he do that to me?" Fresh tears formed, and Lauren shoved them away. At least she had Gwen and Candace. Theirs was a true friendship. "I will not waste my tears on you today, Jeff Levinger." She stomped across the floor, grabbed her things and headed for the shower.

Jeff, Camilla and Lauren had grown up together. "The Three Musketeers," they had dubbed themselves in elementary school. As they had entered high school, Jeff's and Lauren's feelings had changed toward one another. A budding romance had developed, but still they had included Camilla in many of their outings. She was their friend, after all. No one could separate them.

They had made a pact years ago that nothing would ever come between them.

Jeff and Camilla had lied.

As those thoughts filled her mind, Lauren scrubbed herself clean with a vengeance, stepped out of the shower and pulled on a sweat suit.

True, Jeff and Lauren had broken up while in college. She had attended law school in Nevada while Jeff and Camilla had gone to law school in Indiana. The distance had made it impossible for Lauren and Jeff to keep up their relationship. But once she had returned to Indiana after law school, she and Jeff seemed to pick up right where they had left off—or so she had thought.

Please, God, help me to forget him. Help me to forgive them. Even as she prayed those words, she wasn't sure she was ready to let go of her anger.

Lauren scrunched a little gel in her wet hair and lightly dried it. Afterward, she read her morning devotions and had a time of prayer. Next she placed Nocchi in a red checkered gingham dress with a matching bucket hat. Nocchi seemed to enjoy her wardrobe. She never tried to scoot out of the hat or clothes—a dog after Lauren's own heart.

Lauren latched the leash to Nocchi's collar. Deciding she would make a list of what she wanted for her next job, she grabbed her laptop and headed outside to do some work.

Silence met her when she arrived downstairs. How odd. She glanced at her watch. Maybe everyone had gone to church.

She made her way to the kitchen, picked up a muffin and a small bottle of apple juice. A white square piece of paper on the counter caught her attention. "Lauren, after the early church service, we're coming home to change, and then we're going a block down the road to play tennis at a small park area. If you're up to it, come join us. Garrett."

That charmed her—Garrett took his girls to church. She read the note again. Interesting. Did most bed-and-breakfasts plan events for their guests? She had never stayed in one before, so she had no clue. It certainly seemed to offer more than hotels.

Though she appreciated their invitation, she decided to see if she could find a place to think and work a little while. Shoving through the back door, she and Nocchi followed a trail toward the woods. Maybe they'd find a fallen tree or a stump on which she could sit.

The early-afternoon sun sailed brightly overhead warming her face, while a slight breeze moved a few scraps of clouds across the blue sky. Lauren stepped carefully through the yard, noting the green bushes thick with colorful flowers. Not one to have a green thumb, she had no clue as to the names of the flowers, but that didn't stop her from enjoying them. Most floral names she couldn't pronounce anyway. She walked over to a huge pot stuffed with assorted plants of all shapes and varieties. Bending over, she took a deep whiff. "Oh, Nocchi, it's wonderful here." The dog lifted her nose in the air as if trying to catch the scent.

Walking farther on the path into the woods, Lauren stopped when she found a bench. "How great is this?"

Nocchi scanned the area for a moment, then finally settled near Lauren's feet. A lozenge of sunlight draped over the animal's fur, resembling a bright-yellow ribbon. Lauren basked in the scene for a moment, then turned her attention to the laptop. She pulled it from the case and turned it on. Her wireless card didn't work out in the woods, but she didn't need it anyway for what she had to do.

After waiting for everything to boot up, Lauren clicked open a new document in order to make a list of steps to take in her job search once she got home. She stared at the screen, her mind going through the few remaining law firms in town where she hadn't yet sent a resumé. No doubt she would have little luck if her former boss had anything to say about it. True, she had made some huge blunders her last several cases, and true, her mind had been preoccupied with grief over her split with Jeff, but to fire her? Given her meticulous past work record, it seemed a little drastic. She felt sure the fact that one of the senior partners was Jeff's dad entered into play.

Oh, well, it should be easier this way. She wouldn't have to run into Jeff, and when she stopped by, Camilla, in the office anymore.

Maybe she'd do something else. She had enjoyed her prior job; legal work suited her, all right. Still, she couldn't help wondering if there might be another niche for her somewhere. Her parents had worked as attorneys before their retirement. How would they feel if she tried something else? Lauren sighed. She had always figured she'd practice law, raise a family, have a nice house, picket fence, end of story. Unfortunately, her story didn't have a happy ending.

Still, at this point changing her career wasn't really an option. She had bills to pay. After all, it wasn't as though she had a husband's income to fall back on. And things on the horizon didn't appear all that promising—at least as far as a husband was concerned. Who was she kidding? There was *nothing* on the horizon. Not that she cared. Love was too painful—she'd better leave it alone. Feeling her mood take a nosedive, she decided to quit thinking about that and get to work on her list.

One by one she typed the names of law firms in her hometown and the nearest cities that might be a good fit for her. Just for the fun of it, she decided to dream about other things she might do with her life. She enjoyed working with kids, teenagers. Maybe she'd go back to school and get a degree in counseling. She suspected she might enjoy cooking, though she'd never put that theory into practice. Her work kept her far too busy to spend time in the kitchen. Most days she tore open packaged foods and used the microwave, or she went out to eat.

Soon she had quite a number of possibilities typed on a document. Satisfied, she saved the document into a file named "Employment Possibilities." She turned off her computer and snapped it closed, causing Nocchi to glance up. When Lauren moved her head, a pain flared in her neck. Wincing, she wondered how long she had been in the woods. Judging by her stiff neck, it had been a while.

"Working when you should be playing can do that to you," Garrett's voice called from her left.

She turned to him, barely noticing the leap in her heart. Dressed in a polo shirt, khaki shorts, crew socks and gym shoes, he appeared the athletic type. The sweatband across his forehead and tennis racket in his hand added a professional look. "Hi," she said, feeling strangely comforted by his presence.

"Hi, yourself. Okay if I sit down?"

She gestured toward the empty spot beside her.

"Why would anyone bring a laptop to such a restful place? Seems to me you'd want to leave your work behind."

She turned to answer him. His handsome face, mere inches from her, caused her tongue to stick to the roof of her mouth, reminding her of her first day in court. She'd read about those feelings before in books, but she'd never really experienced them. Maybe a few things—fluttering heartbeats, a chill here and there, that kind of thing—with Jeff, but nothing similar to this. Whatever *this* was.

Turning away, she fixed her gaze on the pines. "I was just making a list."

"What kind of a list? Like the Santa Claus kind? You know, making a list, checking it twice?"

She dared a glance and he winked. Lifting a quick grin, she turned away again. She could feel him looking at her still. Call it woman's intuition or the fact that she could almost feel his breath on her cheek—maybe that was wishful thinking on her part—but she felt his gaze on her face.

Which made her remember that she didn't like her profile. She thought her nose was weird. Still, she was proud of herself for resisting the urge to cover it with her hand.

She suddenly remembered she hadn't told him about her job situation. Or more appropriately, lack of one.

"Uh-oh, did I overstep my bounds?"

She wavered about whether she should tell him or not. "No, you're fine," she finally said. "The truth is I lost my job just before I came here."

"Oh?" His eyebrows rose slightly.

"I was just making a list of places that might be a good fit for me. I'm not worried. I have enough money to get by until I find something else."

He nodded but kept silent. They stared into the forest. The wind whispered through the trees. The smell of pine mingled with the musky scent of his cologne and wafted her way. She closed her eyes and breathed in, lingering in the moment.

A comfortable pause stretched between them. "I love this place," he said, barely above a whisper.

Opening her eyes, she cocked her head slightly and peeked at him. He stared at his hands, which were clasped together in his lap. "That's why the bench is here. I love to come out here."

"Oh, I'm sorry." She started to grab her things. "I've infringed upon your private place."

He placed his hand on hers, sending a thousand little tingles up her arm. "Please, don't go." His words were as warm and inviting as his touch.

"The truth is, the guests are all fine, but you're easy to talk to. I mean, I'm usually not this comfortable talking with beautiful women."

Her opinion of him continued to rise.

"I normally keep pretty much to myself, but my daughters seem to enjoy pushing me out of my comfort zone."

"I have a friend who does that—" She corrected herself. "I mean, I had a friend who did that."

"You're not friends anymore?" he asked as if truly interested.

Lauren shook her head. "She betrayed me." Good grief. What had made her tell him that? Now he'd ask her a bunch of questions, and she didn't want to talk about it. Besides, it was none of his business.

"Oh, I'm sorry" was all he said. "It's hard to lose the people we love." He looked down.

"Your wife?"

He nodded.

"Now I'm sorry."

He paused a moment. "I guess we have to move past those things, right? That's what they tell us, anyway."

"Yeah, I guess they do," she said, recalling Candace and Gwen's advice. Lauren decided this man was nice. In fact, he was better than nice. He seemed genuine, kind, a good father. And the fact that he sort of resembled George Clooney didn't hurt either. She lifted a prayer that God would bless Garrett Cantrell.

"Well, I didn't mean to intrude on your work time, Lauren. Just happened by and saw you, wanted to say hello."

This time there was no mistaking how her heart leaped when he said her name. What was up with that? It wasn't as though she was interested or anything. She was lonely—and, well, she *had* seen most of George Clooney's movies. That's all it was.

"I'm glad you stopped by. I need to head back anyway. Can you recommend a good restaurant for lunch?"

His eyes brightened. "Hey, this isn't on the schedule, but the girls don't have me committed until tonight anyway. Want to have lunch with me?"

Lauren hadn't a clue what he was talking about, but she didn't want to pry. "Sure, that would be great," she said, meaning it.

"Good," he answered. He carried her laptop for her and together they headed back toward the house. "I'm really glad you came, Lauren."

There was that heart flip again. He'd better quit saying her name or she'd need a pacemaker before the two weeks were over. She shot a glance his way. "Me, too." Though she hardly knew this man, she felt a strange connection with him. Maybe because they'd both endured heartache. And then there was that whole George Clooney thing. She didn't know.

But one thing she did know—the idea of spending the next couple of weeks at the Woods Inn Bed and Breakfast sounded pretty good to her right about now.

Chapter Four

When Garrett and Lauren returned from lunch, a van from Channel 4 was situated in the parking lot, and a young reporter was taping an interview with Macy and Molly. Garrett did not have a good feeling about this at all. He groaned.

"You okay?" Lauren asked.

"If I had remained childless I would be okay," he said, shoving the gearshift into Park. Without another word he turned off the engine and jumped out of the car.

How could the girls get him into such a mess? It was one thing to have the stupid contest, but did the whole town have to know about it? No doubt he would never hear the end of it. He reminded himself to be friendly. This was free advertisement for the B and B. Enjoy the process, right? He swallowed the anger that lodged in his throat.

His girls saw him and waved. The reporter, a young man who appeared all of sixteen, turned to him. "Mr. Cantrell, I presume?"

Garrett gave a short tip of his head.

"My name is Drew Huntington, and I'm from News Channel 4. I've been interviewing your daughters about the 'Win Daddy's Heart' contest."

There was the sound of approaching footsteps, and Garrett turned to see the surprise on Lauren's face.

"And you must be one of the contestants?" the reporter asked, his face resembling a puppy about to pounce on a rubber ball. By this kid's eagerness, Garrett figured him to be fresh out of college and new on the job.

"I—" Lauren stopped, her gaze traveling to each one.

Her face turned a shade of white that Garrett had never before seen on a noncelestial being. "Lauren, are you okay?" he asked.

"If you'll excuse me, I'm not feeling so well." With that, she practically ran across the parking lot toward the house.

Garrett turned back to the reporter. "Stage fright," he said to ease the tension, though his stomach churned, not buying his own story for a moment.

Everyone laughed. The reporter talked to each of them awhile, getting the information on how Macy and Molly had come up with the idea, the names of the contestants, where they were from and any incidental details they had given the girls.

"So you don't know much about Lauren, is that right?"

Macy shook her head. "We've misplaced her application. We can find out for you, though."

Drew Huntington perked up. "Great. I can come back." His eyes locked with Macy's. She blushed beneath his gaze. Garrett saw the whole thing and didn't like it one little bit. He cleared his throat.

Drew turned to Garrett. "I think this is fun news, Mr. Cantrell. A human interest story not just for Bliss Village residents. It might even be picked up by the big guys."

Garrett's gut twisted. His icy gaze settled upon his daughters. Molly coughed. Macy's right eye twitched again.

Confusion registered on Drew's face, and he fingered the collar of his shirt. "Yes, well, I'll let you folks get back to your contest." He handed his camera to the other man with him and quickly made arrangements with Macy to drop back in the middle of the week to talk further with the contestants. He said goodbye to Garrett and Molly. He turned to say goodbye to Macy. "Nice to meet you," he said, extending his hand. With nary a twitch, both eyes sparkled as she looked at him, his hand holding hers a little longer than necessary.

Garrett folded his arms across his chest and frowned. "Girls, we need to think about dinner preparations." His voice was deeper and stronger than usual. His lips pulled into a thin line and he glared at Macy.

She defiantly stared back. "We just ate lunch."

"*I'm* hungry," he snapped, though that wasn't exactly accurate. He had eaten a late lunch with Lauren.

The reporter scurried off to his van, took one last glance at Macy and flashed a huge grin before he climbed aboard.

Garrett wanted to string the little twerp up by his toenails.

He and his eldest daughter were having enough problems getting along without throwing a boy into the mix just before she heads off to college. She had her mind on a college degree, and he aimed to see she kept it there.

Macy smiled until the van faded from view. When she turned to Garrett, the corners of her mouth drooped south. "What was that all about?" The hands on her hips told him she was prepared for a fight.

"He was just being nice, Dad," Molly interjected.

Garrett's head jerked toward his youngest. "You stay out of this, Molly."

She promptly closed her mouth and headed for the house.

"Listen, Macy—"

"No, you listen, Dad. I'm not a little girl anymore. I know you're lonely. I know you miss Mom, but things are what they are. We can't bring her back. And I can't stay with you forever. Neither can Molly. We have our own lives to live!" She turned and ran into the house.

Garrett felt as though he'd been punched in the gut. Was that what this contest was about? The girls thought they had to get him someone so they could have their own lives? Did they really think they needed to take care of him?

He walked to his bench in the back woods, speaking quietly to his wife. "I've made such a mess of things, Susie. I don't know how to do this." His jaw tensed as he waited for the words. "Why did you leave me? I don't want to do this by myself!" The sharp pain of guilt stabbed him, making him ache all over. "I meant to get that tire fixed! Oh, how I meant to get it fixed." His mind agonized with the thought of her tire blowing, causing her to lose control of the car and plow into a utility pole. His words twisted in agony, then snuffed to silence as he allowed the familiar thorns of guilt to tear into his conscience and pierce his momentary peace once again. "God, I need Your help."

Garrett swallowed hard. He hadn't called upon God since before Susie's death. Weakness made him do so now. He lifted a determined jaw and pulled in a ragged breath. No. God had turned a deaf ear when Garrett had needed Him most.

Garrett would not turn to Him now. He would take the girls to church for Susie's sake, but that's as far as he would go.

Standing, Garrett headed toward the house, all the while ignoring the empty shadow that hovered over his heart.

Lauren closed her door and fell onto the bed. "A contest?" Staring into space, she felt the truth hit her like a bad jury decision. "The surprise!" She smacked her palm against her forehead. "I'm such an idiot! How did I forget the surprise?"

She stood and began to pace. So that's why everyone had thought she wasn't coming. She must have been late or something. A contest to win *his* heart. What had Candace and Gwen been thinking? She felt near hysteria. The last thing she wanted was another romantic involvement. For crying out loud, couldn't they see how Jeff had hurt her? How could they put her through that again? She continued to pace. She needed a gym, time to think. It always helped her to work out when she was upset. She skidded to a halt and looked at Nocchi. "We'll go for a brisk walk in the woods—

without the laptop. The fresh air will be better than being inside a gym, anyway."

Adrenaline pushing her forward, Lauren gathered Nocchi and headed for the woods at a record pace. Even though there wasn't a path, she wandered deep into the dense pines. Jeff had told her she was a work-aholic and needed to loosen up, enjoy life a little. Maybe she should prove to him—to everyone—she could enjoy life as well as the next person. Though she wasn't interested in romantic involvement with anyone at this point, it couldn't hurt to play along in the game. And she didn't want to disappoint Gwen and Candace. Or Molly and Macy, for that matter.

As thoughts of the contest bounced around in her mind, she came to a tree that bore the initials *GC* plus *SC* with a heart around it. Lauren stopped and traced the markings with her fingers. Garrett and his wife. How he must grieve for her still. Lauren's heart ached for that kind of love.

Thoughts of her life, her future mingled with her raw emotions. Macy and Molly, and Garrett and a wife Lauren could not visualize. What a precious family they must have been. Lauren wondered if anyone could ever love her that way. She whispered a prayer for the Cantrells and one for herself. How hard it was to trust God with a future she could not see. A future she felt sure held only loneliness.

When she finally pulled free from her thoughts, Lauren scanned the area, feeling she had gone a little farther into the forest than she had planned. With a glimpse upward, Lauren noticed that the tiny opening beyond the treetops revealed dark, low-hanging clouds. "Hmm, it might rain, Nocchi. We'd better get to the house."

Lifting the dog into her arms, Lauren started back. After walking a while, she came to the same marking on the tree that she had seen earlier. If a sliver of panic had not rushed through her, she might have gotten excited with the realization that Garrett and George Clooney had the same initials. Unfortunately, even that couldn't lift her spirits now. She was lost.

"Let's see. The sun rises in the east and sets in the west." Nocchi cocked her head to look at Lauren. "Don't be impressed. I have absolutely no idea whatsoever what that has to do with me finding our way back to the house."

She'd be the first to admit her friends were right about her being directionally challenged. She figured some people had brown eyes, some had blue. Some came equipped with an internal compass, some didn't.

She didn't.

Lauren stood a moment and tried to get her bearings. The trees started to rustle overhead, a sure sign a storm was brewing.

An urgency pushed her to get back to the house. She began to jog. Her speed picked up with the wind, her steps taking her one direction, then another, then another. Rain began to fall from the sky and pelted her skin. A chill worked its way to her bones. Nocchi shivered in Lauren's arms. She wanted to cry, but refused to give in to her emotions. Her body grew cold and wet as her tired legs ran hard through the wooded maze. Limbs swayed overhead. She thought she heard a man's voice call out, but decided it must be the sound of the whipping wind that howled through the trees.

Water dripped from Lauren's hair onto her face. A

shadow moved ahead of her. She wiped her eyes to see if she had imagined it. Another movement. With everything stirring around her, it was hard to tell if it was a tree or something else. It could even be a bear. Faster and faster she ran the other way, her feet sloshing through puddles, her vision blurred. A pain cramped in her side. The cold pierced her lungs. There was that voice again. Was it Garrett's? As she slowed to catch her breath, a hand clamped upon her arm. "Lauren!"

A gasp caught in her throat. Fear froze her in place. Lauren stood trembling when the owner of the hand stepped around her into view. She peered through wet lashes to see concern etched on Garrett Cantrell's face. "Are you okay? You were gone so long. I was worried about you. Since I didn't hear Nocchi in your room when I knocked on your door, I figured you took her into the woods."

Without hesitation she fell against him, exhausted from running, chilled from the rain. He dropped his umbrella and pulled her so tightly against him, she could feel his heart beating through his light jacket. Her mind muddied like the ground beneath her feet. How long she stood locked in his embrace she didn't know. She didn't care. Finally he leaned back so that he could see her, still holding her in his arms. "I'd better get you to the house so you can change into some warm clothes," he said, but his feet stayed planted, his eyes probing deeply into hers.

Feeling his breath brush lightly against her cheeks made her light-headed. She was afraid to breathe, afraid of breaking the stillness between them. Her legs wobbled. Suddenly Nocchi shivered in Lauren's arms, bringing Lauren and Garrett both back to their senses.

Dumb dog. Should have left her in the room.

Garrett picked up the umbrella and held it over them while edging Lauren out of the woods. She realized she probably never would have found her way back without him.

Once they were back at the house, she ran upstairs, peeled off her drenched clothes down to the skin and pulled on a sweatshirt and pair of jeans, then dried her hair. She also dried Nocchi, then left her in the bedroom and returned downstairs. But for the soft violin music playing from the stereo, the house was quiet as she slipped into the front room, where a cozy fire played in the hearth. Garrett entered carrying two cups of steaming liquid on a tray.

"I guess Macy and Molly took the ladies sightseeing. They try to give me little breaks here and there. It appears we have the house to ourselves."

Adrenaline surged through her body.

"Though I seriously doubt they'll stay gone long in this weather. Not exactly a great day for sightseeing," he added. "I know you drink coffee, so I made some." He placed the tray of coffee cups, sugar and cream on the table. He stood and handed her a cup. "Want some sugar or cream?

"Sugar," she answered, thinking how nice it was to be in this room with Garrett Cantrell. Reminded her of a scene out of a movie.

Garrett gave her some sugar and a spoon, then grabbed his own cup and sat down beside her on the sofa near the fireplace.

"I'm sorry you had to go out," she said, stirring sugar into her coffee, then taking a sip. "I didn't realize I could get lost in the woods. I feel so foolish." Truth was she could get lost a mile from home. She placed her cup on the table.

His expression held apology. "Don't feel that way. It's easy to get lost in the woods, especially if you're not familiar with the area." He took a drink of coffee. "I thought you seemed upset with that news reporter. In fact, you almost appeared surprised, as if you didn't know about the contest."

She took a deep breath. "Well, as a matter of fact, Garrett, I didn't know about the contest."

Confusion flickered in his eyes. "How is that possible? Aren't you the fifth contestant?"

Lauren laughed. "Well, I guess I am, but you see, my friends set this up for me." She explained how Gwen and Candace had encouraged her to come to the bed-and-breakfast, take a break, and that they had said a surprise awaited her there.

Garrett chuckled. He settled back against the cushions and stretched his arm across the top of the sofa, his fingers hovering a mere half inch from her shoulder. "I guess we both got surprised." He explained how the girls had set up the contest, and he'd known nothing about it until it was too late to stop it.

"I hope you don't mind being here now." His eyes searched hers.

Big brown, soft, compelling eyes—eyes that made her heart turn liquid. "No, it's been, um, kind of fun up to now."

At this Garrett laughed out loud. "Kind of fun? Well, I guess that's one way to view it," he said.

"No, I didn't mean that I wasn't enjoying—"

He scooted in a bit and placed his hand on her shoulder, giving her a light squeeze. "I know you didn't. It's okay. I'm just glad you came," he said, his eyes locking with hers. Her shoulder warmed to his touch. The soft music floating overhead, the tenderness of his hand resting on her shoulder made her want to close her eyes and imagine him lifting his fingers to her hair—

Suddenly Garrett pulled his hand away as if he had been burned. The sleepy haze that had settled over her disappeared like a mirage in the desert.

"Everyone should be back soon." He got up and walked toward the window. Pulling back the curtain, he peeked out, then dropped the cloth back into place and turned toward her.

Lauren lifted her cup to her lips. Anything to cover the awkward moment between them. She didn't want to analyze what had just happened. The image of the carved initials on the tree came to mind, reaffirming her conclusion that he was still grieving for his wife.

Lauren curled her feet beneath her on the sofa. "So tell me about your girls. How do they feel about living in a bed-and-breakfast?"

He looked relieved that Lauren had changed the subject. He returned to his place beside her, but she didn't miss the fact that he sat farther away this time. "I think they're okay with it. Sometimes I think it infringes on their privacy, but they've adjusted pretty well."

"And how are they since they've lost their mother?" Lauren asked in almost a whisper. Not that it was any of her business, but she had noticed a little friction between Macy and her dad.

A shadow touched his face. "As well as can be expected, I guess." He raked his fingers through his hair. "Macy's the hard one. I think she blames me."

Lauren's heart squeezed. "Oh, I'm sure that's not true."

He blew out a heavy sigh. "I don't know. When Susie died, Macy changed."

"It would be hard on a girl to lose her mother."

"That's true enough. But Molly's adjusted. She has her moments, but she doesn't pick at me all the time."

"I know plenty of girls who pick at their parents. It's an age thing, I think. I'm sure I did." She laughed.

Garrett lifted a hopeful expression to Lauren. "Maybe you're right. I just know the sooner we get past it, the better." They heard a car door close. "That must be them."

Before they could get up, Macy and the others swished through the front door and stepped into the front room.

Garrett rose from the couch and turned to greet them.

Gracie locked eyes with Lauren. "Well, looky here. Ain't this just so cozy?" She walked across the room and looked from Lauren to Garrett, her words dripping with insincerity. She glanced down at the coffee tray and turned to the other contestants. "I guess while we've been sightseeing, Lucy here has been having a good time of her own."

Shock kept Lauren silent.

"I don't know what you mean by that, Gracie, but I invited Lauren to sit down with me for coffee. Is there a problem with that?" Garrett's eyes pinned her.

She lifted her face with a look of total innocence. "Why, no, Garrett, not at all. Anything you want, you get." She flashed her pearly-white teeth.

"Hey, would you ladies want some hot chocolate?" Molly offered, clearly trying to defuse the situation.

"Great idea. I'll go put my things upstairs and be back," Billie Gibbons said, making her way up the stairs.

"Yeah, me, too." Nikki Spartan tossed them her Elvis smile. Lauren could almost hear strains of "You Ain't Nothin' but a Hound Dog."

Ellen Little followed along behind them, hands clenched together, mouth tightly sealed. She looked so fragile Lauren feared that if someone blew on her, she would break into a thousand pieces.

Garrett went to help Molly and Macy get hot chocolate for the guests, leaving Lauren and Gracie alone in the room.

Gracie lifted an arched brow and glared at Lauren. "Don't think I'm not onto you, honey. You might as well know right here and now, *I am* winning this contest." With that, she turned and walked from the room, allowing her chin to lead the way.

Little did Gracie know that if Lauren had had any doubts about being a contestant before, she didn't now. She knew a challenge when she heard one.

Suddenly the idea of being a contestant in this game suited her just fine.

Chapter Five

Monday evening after dinner Lauren went up to her room and settled onto her bed. It had been a good day of everyone getting to know one another. Macy and Molly had planned an afternoon of games and refreshments, and Lauren had to admit she'd truly enjoyed herself.

As a matter of fact, Lauren figured that for the next couple of weeks she could pretty much get along with everyone there—well, she might struggle the teensiest bit with Gracie. Then again, this could be the challenge of a lifetime. Lauren sighed. She supposed Gracie could be nice when she wanted to. Obviously she didn't want to. Gracie needed to get over her attitude.

First of all, Lauren hadn't even known about the contest when she first arrived, and secondly, the last thing she wanted was another romantic entanglement. Her life had enough stress without adding that to the mix.

Hearing a car door close outside, Lauren hurried over to her window and peeked out the curtains. Today marked the beginning of Garrett meeting with the contestants individually. He was taking Ellen out tonight.

With Ellen settled into her seat, Garrett walked over to the driver's side of his car. Lauren bit on the corner of her lip. For a tiny moment, similar to a blip on a computer screen, Lauren wished she were the one going with Garrett tonight. The thought irritated her.

Nocchi whined, causing Lauren to turn. "I know I'm being utterly ridiculous. I couldn't care less that he's taking these women out. It's a stupid contest, and that's what he's supposed to do. It's just that Gracie has turned this into a competition, and, well, I don't want to sit back and let her win, do I?" Maybe it was the lawyer in her.

Speechless, Nocchi cocked her head sideways and stared at Lauren. Yeah, they had moments like that. Where Lauren talked and Nocchi listened. Smart dog. Too bad people weren't the same.

Even as Lauren spoke the words, she had a sneaking suspicion there was more to her motive than just a competitive streak, but she could not allow herself to explore that possibility. Not yet. She wasn't ready. She still had to shake her feelings for Jeff Levinger.

Lauren plopped onto the bed. "Why did Candace and Gwen get me into this mess, Nocchi?" Tail wagging, the dog stood on her hind legs, scratching to get on the bed.

Lauren lifted the now clothesless pooch onto the high mattress. "Nobody understands me the way you do." She nuzzled her nose into Nocchi's fur and cuddled her. "Nocchi, what am I going to do? I don't want to be here. I don't want to be a part of this contest. I just want a job, and a new life."

Nocchi stretched out beside Lauren, nestling in close to her side. Lauren absently stroked her dog. Her restless thoughts finally surrendered to heavy eyelids as she drifted off to sleep.

A while later a car door slammed outside, causing Lauren to wake up. She lifted her head with a start, feeling somewhat disoriented. Reality hit her like a splash from Lake Tahoe. She was at a B and B vying for the affections of a man she hardly knew. Why? For one thing, to please her friends who had gone through all the trouble to get her there. Secondly? She had been pushed aside by one woman already in the past six months.

She wasn't about to move over again.

Wait. The stakes weren't the same—were they? It's not as though she was in love with Garrett Cantrell, after all. Her chin rose. Still, she would not step aside. Lauren's friends wanted her to win—what was the prize again? Hadn't the reporter called the contest "Win Daddy's Heart"? Well, she didn't want the entanglement any more than Garrett did, but she could at least enjoy the adventure. That would show Jeff Levinger and Camilla Renfrow a thing or two.

Lauren walked over and peeked out the window. Garrett and Ellen had returned. Neither looked very happy.

When Garrett and Ellen stepped into the house, Macy and Molly looked at them with hope in their eyes. Garrett was not a happy camper. Not even a happy B and B owner. In fact, he was beginning to think that the whole dad thing was way overrated.

"Good night, Garrett," Ellen croaked in barely a whisper, her glasses slipping down her nose. She cleared her throat and pushed her spectacles back into place.

"Good night, Ellen," he said, much as he would talk to a child. When her back was turned toward the stairs, he motioned for his daughters to follow him into the den. They obeyed. Closing the door behind them, Garrett walked over in front of the sofa where they sat.

"Didn't it go well?" Macy was the first to ask.

"That's the understatement of the year, Macy." He ran his fingers through his hair. "And I have far too many days left of this."

"I don't get it. We had the contestants fill out a personality profile and they all seemed to match with your likes and dislikes," Molly said.

"I think some of them didn't answer honestly," Macy added.

"Bingo!" Garrett said with far too much attitude.

"We're sorry, Dad. We thought we were doing a good thing, but you're not enjoying it," Molly said. She looked down at the floor, her expression forlorn, disappointed.

He hated it when she did that. Got to him every time. "Look, girls, I appreciate your efforts, but this just isn't me. When I meet a woman, it will be unplanned, just something that happens, and I'll let nature take its course." He thought of Lauren and, not ready to deal with what that meant, quickly pushed her from his thoughts.

Molly brightened. "What about Gracie and Lauren? You seem to enjoy them. Or maybe one of the other women?"

Molly, his bold, tenacious one. When she got an

idea, she clenched it as tight as Bear with a steak bone. "They're nice ladies, but I don't know. Gracie talks too much, and though I enjoy being around Lauren, we're as different as night and day."

"How so?" Molly probed.

"She's, well…citified. Actually takes her laptop into the woods."

"What's wrong with that? Better than sitting at a stuffy old desk," Molly argued.

He stared at her. "You don't get it. The point of going into the woods is to relax. You reflect, rest, rejuvenate. Kind of hard to do with a laptop."

"Everyone is different, Dad. Doesn't mean you can't have a relationship with someone with diverse interests."

"Have you seen the way she dresses that dog?"

The girls laughed. "I think it's kind of cute," Molly said.

Garrett glared at her. "Lauren's uncomfortable here. She's like an exquisite piece of fine china in a flea market." He didn't enjoy explaining himself to his daughters. He had his reasons—let that be enough. His heart clenched. Okay, so he owed them that much. They had gone to a lot of trouble to pull this contest together. Still, they should have run it by him first.

"She's only been here a couple of days, Dad. Give it time."

"By the way—" he looked at them incredulously "—how could you possibly think I'd be interested in a Nikki Spartan type?"

Macy and Molly shared a glance. "Um, we're not sure how that slipped past us, Dad. Her picture was much tamer than her actual, uh, appearance."

"Yeah, she wasn't wearing black in the picture," Molly added.

"Besides, you shouldn't judge her by her outer appearance." Macy lifted a defiant chin.

She was right, of course. Garrett rubbed his forehead. He could feel a headache coming on. The last thing he needed tonight was to deal with his rebellious firstborn. Couldn't they carry on a single conversation without some sort of conflict? He was at a loss as to how to handle her. Did she blame him? Maybe she had heard him talking to Susie about getting the tire repaired. Maybe Macy knew he hadn't gotten around to it. The rest was history. His neglect had caused Susie's death. He had tried to get the car in for repair and their mechanic hadn't been able to get to it for a couple of days. Still, Garrett should have gone somewhere else or forbidden Susie to drive it. Not that she would have listened to him. She'd had a mind of her own.

Macy resembled her mother in many ways.

Molly's voice pulled him from the painful past. "At least give them all a chance, will you, Dad? You might be pleasantly surprised," she said perkily.

Glancing from Molly to Macy, he released a sigh. As long as he had his girls, he couldn't stay down long. "I'll give them a chance. But once the two weeks are over, you girls owe me. Big-time."

Molly squealed and hugged him. Macy dared to smile. "Now go to bed, you knuckleheads," he said with a laugh.

His eyes locked with Macy's. "Night, Mace."

She seemed to weaken for just a moment. A softness touched her face. "Night, Dad." He wanted to run to her, hold her, tell her they could get through this and everything would be all right, but just as quickly as it had come, the softness faded and her body stiffened as she turned and walked toward the door with determined steps.

That same night, Lauren's stomach growled and she realized she had slept through dinner. She didn't feel like going out this late. Maybe she would go downstairs for an apple or some little snack. Glancing at her sleeping dog, Lauren edged her way out of the room.

She was hungry, that was all, she told herself all the way down the stairs, ignoring completely any other motives that might possibly send her downstairs at this late hour.

When she reached the bottom stair, she waited and listened for a moment. Nothing.

Just then the door to the den opened and soon Garrett, Macy and Molly stood at the entrance to the front room. They looked surprised to see Lauren.

"I'm sorry, I was kind of hungry. I hadn't eaten dinner—fell asleep, actually, and I thought I might grab something..." Lauren's face felt hot.

The girls smiled. Garrett just looked at her. She didn't know what else to say, so she turned to go.

"Lauren, wait."

She whirled, her heart flipping again at the sound of Garrett speaking her name.

"I'll see what we've got. Maybe I can fix you something." He turned back to Macy and Molly. "Good night, girls."

Lauren didn't miss the amusement on their faces, nor

did she miss the face Garrett made at them. They giggled, and he turned his attention back to Lauren.

Lauren felt Garrett's hand brush against the small of her back in a tiny nudge as they slipped through the kitchen entrance. His touch was so slight, so quick, she wondered if she had imagined it.

"You really don't need to fix me anything, Garrett. I was just going to grab some fruit or something."

"How about some pie and decaf coffee? Macy made one for lunch and there are still a couple of pieces left."

"That sounds pretty good. Thanks."

He grinned. "Hey, we aim to please at Woods Inn Bed and Breakfast."

Lauren smiled.

"Can I help you?" she asked.

"No, I can handle this. You just grab a seat at the table."

Lauren complied and watched Garrett as he made the coffee, filled the dessert dishes with pie and a dollop of whipped cream, then brought everything to the table.

"This looks wonderful," Lauren said. A warm shiver ran through her as she watched Garrett place the plates and silverware on the table and pour their coffee.

Lauren whispered a prayer over her pie and they started eating.

Her gaze went out the window at the lights flooding the back lawn.

"Nice night, huh?" Garrett commented, his unwavering gaze taking in every inch of her face—or at least, that's what it seemed to her.

Another shiver swept down her spine. She turned away. "I love the summer. And what could be more wonderful than this place? The mountains, the stars, the moon—" She stopped herself when she saw him staring at her again.

"Don't stop. Your eyes twinkle when you talk," Garrett said, reaching up as if he would brush his finger against her cheek. Lauren took a quick breath, and he quickly brought his hand down before he made contact.

Feeling a little awkward, Lauren went back to her pie and Garrett did the same.

Just then they heard footsteps at the kitchen door, causing them to look up. Gracie stood there pouting.

"You're having apple pie without me?"

Lauren noticed Garrett's face looked a little flushed. He quickly stood. "I'm sorry, Gracie. Would you like some?"

"Oh, no, thank you, Garrett. I was only teasing. *I* have to watch *my* figure, you know." She threw Lauren a fleeting glance, then looked back at Garrett. "But I do have a problem."

"Oh?"

"The light in my room isn't working right, and I wondered if you could take a look?" Her eyelashes fluttered like the end of a tape on a movie reel.

"Well, I—"

"Please? After all, you have finished your pie," she said sweetly.

"Uh…" He looked at Lauren.

"You go ahead, Garrett. I'm almost done, too. By the way, thank you for the pie."

"You're welcome."

Before he could get another word in, Gracie tucked her arm into Garrett's. "You're just the sweetest thing,

Garrett, honey. Thank you for doing this. I just can't get to sleep unless I read at night, and I couldn't read with the light not working and all." She lifted a triumphant smile to Lauren, then nuzzled closer to Garrett as they made their way out of the kitchen.

Lauren watched her, amazed that the woman was taking this contest so seriously. She sat there a little longer, then heard a voice behind her.

"Hi."

Lauren turned to see Macy.

"I was coming down for some juice before bed when I saw Dad leave with Gracie." She walked over to the refrigerator, pulled out some orange juice and poured it into a glass. "What's that all about? I thought you and Dad were talking."

"She was having problems with a light or something," Lauren said.

"Mind if I sit down?"

"Please do," Lauren said, feeling a bit amused. Close to eleven-thirty at night and she was being interviewed by Garrett's daughter. Oddly enough, she didn't mind. In fact, she thought it was sweet how his daughters were trying to take care of him, probably trying to tie up loose ends before they both headed off to college.

"It sure was sweet of you and Molly to throw this contest for your dad."

Macy grunted. "I wish Dad thought so. He just wants to get it over."

"Oh?" For some reason that comment bothered Lauren.

"I'm sorry. It's not that he isn't enjoying all of you. He just—"

"You don't need to explain, Macy," Lauren said, feeling a little disappointed.

"Dad doesn't want to be pushed into anything. And, well, he feels that we are pushing him to pick someone."

"And are you?"

"Not really. If you remember the contest rules, we said nothing was guaranteed except that you would have a two-week vacation at our B and B with free food and lodging. The romance thing is just a plus—if it happens."

Lauren explained that her friends had gotten her into the contest.

"Really? I don't remember your entry," Macy said. She paused a moment. "'Course, it's been a while since we've seen the entry. We lost it."

"Oh."

"So tell me about you," Macy said.

Let the interview begin. Lauren explained about her work as an attorney, and the fact that she had lost her job. Macy talked about her graduation and how much she missed her mom not being there.

"Dad pretty much has stayed to himself, just running the B and B since Mom died."

"I'm so sorry, Macy." Lauren didn't know what else to say.

"We manage." She waited a moment. "I'm surprised someone as pretty as you hasn't married before now," she said, changing the subject.

Lauren was a little surprised at Macy's bold assessment, but the innocence on her face showed she didn't mean anything by it. "Well, Macy, it's this way. I waited until I was settled in a career before I got engaged."

Macy's eyes widened. "You were engaged? What happened?"

Lauren found Macy's curiosity amusing. "One night I returned to the office for a while to get some work done. I didn't know my fiancé was working. I wrote him a note and went in to place it on his desk. When I entered his office, he was standing there kissing my best friend."

Macy gasped. "How awful!"

Lauren was surprised that she could talk about it so freely, and even more amazed that she felt no pain with the mention of it. "I thought it was pretty awful at the time, but I'm okay with it now. See, we had been the best of friends from the time we were kids, and it just seemed natural to eventually end up together. But now I'm beginning to think that's all we ever were—friends."

Just then they heard a shoe scuffle on the floor behind them. They turned around with a start.

"Oh, excuse me," Gracie said. "I thought your dad might have come back down here. I needed to ask him something else." With that she turned and left.

"Wonder what that was all about," Macy said, watching her.

"Who knows?" Lauren felt a little uncomfortable that Gracie had overheard their conversation. Not that it mattered. It didn't really make any difference if Gracie knew that Lauren had been engaged.

Still, Lauren couldn't deny the uneasy feeling churning in her stomach....

Exhausted, Garrett could hardly wait to slip between the sheets. His date with Ellen had been a total bust. She was pretty in a shy, soft kind of way, but when they went to dinner he practically had to pry every word out of her. Once they returned to his car, she had burst into tears and told him she didn't want to be there, but since she hadn't had a vacation from her library job in a couple of years, and she didn't have a lot of vacation money, her mom and sister had made her come. He'd assured her everything was all right, and she could stay for the duration of the two weeks. He wouldn't pressure her. He'd confessed he didn't want to do the contest either.

They had passed the rest of the evening in a theater watching a movie. In silence. He figured he could throw her a book or two and she'd be all set for the time remaining in the contest.

One down, four to go.

"Two weeks," he told himself as he crawled into bed. His head sank into the pillow, and he moved around until he was comfortable. "Less than that now," he encouraged himself, his mind drifting to his time with Lauren in the kitchen. The way she looked under the soft glow of lamplight.

Not wanting to think about it, he punched his pillow into place once more. Before long, he felt himself drift into the hazy world where dreams are made—and barely noticed when Lauren Romey slipped into his mind's view, edging her way ever so close to his heart....

Chapter Six

Lauren took a deep breath before stepping into the dining room to join the other contestants for breakfast.

"Well, hello, sleepyhead," Billie said before stuffing a bite of cinnamon roll into her mouth.

All eyes turned to Lauren. Billie had all the finesse of a backwoods hunter, but Lauren enjoyed her. Still, Lauren guessed if she entered the room in a fur coat, Billie would have Lauren pinned to the floor before she knew what hit her.

"Good morning." Lauren looked around the room. She stopped when her eyes locked with Gracie's. Refusing intimidation, Lauren held her gaze. For crying out loud, she thought, Gracie acted as though it was a matter of life and death to win the contest. With her looks, she should have no problem finding a man, so what was the deal?

"Hey," Nikki said, breaking Lauren's stare-off with Gracie.

"Hi," Lauren said. She grabbed a plate and began to

gather some food. Ellen sat quietly nearby. Lauren turned to her. "Good morning." She knew full well Ellen would never exchange a word with anyone if not forced into conversation.

Ellen's gaze flickered up at Lauren, then quickly back to her plate. "Morning." She pushed her eyeglasses up the bridge of her nose, then coughed before picking up her glass of water. The ice cubes tinkled softly as she took a drink with shaky hands.

The woman could use an antianxiety med. Just being around her made Lauren nervous.

"Sugar, you should get those glasses adjusted so they don't fall all the time," Gracie said.

Ellen looked up. "Well, um, I usually wear contacts, but I've been having some allergy problems and they made my eyes itch."

Gracie tossed a look at Ellen that said she was a total loser.

Okay, Ellen might be a little shy, but there was no use making her feel worse, Lauren thought.

"I was thinking how nice those glasses are, Ellen. They make you look very chic," Lauren said.

She brightened. "Really?"

"Yes, really," Lauren said, meaning it. Ellen had a very innocent quality about her, and her gentle appearance only added to her charm. Unfortunately, she seemed to hold everyone at arm's length, no doubt making it difficult for her establish any meaningful relationships.

Lauren glanced toward the kitchen, wondering if Garrett and the girls were in there.

"They're gone, ain't it a shame? The girls went to

breakfast with some friends, and Garrett rushed off to the store. It's just us little ol' contestants," Gracie said, batting her eyelashes a couple of times for Southern emphasis.

Lauren could almost imagine a decorative handheld fan fluttering in front of Gracie's porcelain face. Lauren stopped her vision short of snatching the imaginary fan and whacking the Southern belle over the head with it.

Gracie clapped her hands with gusto. "I get to go out with Garrett next," she said, keeping her eyes fixed on Lauren.

"That's nice," Lauren said, trying to remain civil.

"He sure is a looker, I'll give him that," Billie said, tearing into a hunk of sausage.

"Ain't he, though," Gracie said, her right eyebrow arched, chin lifted. "I 'spect we'll have a mighty fine time together."

There was that triumphant grin again. Lauren could almost feel the smoke coming from her ears. Time to pray. Gracie worked Lauren's prayer bones the way a torture bed worked its victim.

The back door opened and footsteps sounded in the kitchen. Garrett came to the dining-room entrance. "Morning, ladies," he said, his eyes stopping at Lauren.

"Good morning, Garrett," Gracie quickly called, pulling his glance her way.

"These cinnamon rolls sure are good," Billie said between bites.

"They rock," Nikki chimed in.

Garrett and Lauren exchanged a glance. Lauren looked down at her plate, then over at Gracie, who made it perfectly clear she wasn't happy.

"Thanks. Guess I'll have to try one. Macy and Molly made those."

"You're kidding," Lauren said. "These are wonderful. Where did they learn to cook?" As soon as the words were out of her mouth, she wished she hadn't said them.

"Their mother," Garrett said before disappearing back into the kitchen.

"Oh, that was real good. Bring up the dead wife," Gracie groused in a whisper.

"Well, I didn't—"

"You can't pretend she didn't live," Billie defended.

Ellen kept her nose pointed south, causing her glasses to fall into her plate. She picked them up, wiped the sausage grease off them with her napkin and slipped them back on without ever making eye contact with anyone else.

Nikki jumped in. "Yeah, it's not as though there aren't reminders everywhere. Her pictures in the hallway, her—"

"He ought to take those down," Gracie snapped. "It ain't healthy."

Lauren was sorry she had mentioned anything at all.

"Well, pipe down—here he comes," Billie said, a fraction before he came into the dining room.

Garrett picked up a plate and piled on some breakfast. The room stayed silent but for the clatter of forks against earthenware.

"So, Garrett honey, where are we going on our date?" Gracie asked, her sweet voice back in place.

"I'll talk to you about it after breakfast," he said, dismissing the matter entirely. He went back to the kitchen for something.

Lauren noticed he seemed uncomfortable. She figured he couldn't wait until the entire ordeal was over. Not that she could blame him. This wasn't exactly the restful time she had expected either.

"Boy, I sure miss the big-city lights back home. This place is so boring," Nikki said, glancing toward the kitchen. Lauren figured Nikki didn't want Garrett to overhear her comments.

"Where are you from again?" Lauren asked, pouring a cup of coffee. "I know Garrett told me when he introduced you, but I'm sorry, I've forgotten."

"San Francisco."

"This is definitely different than San Francisco. You should live where I live. The nearest grocery is twenty miles away. But we got elk and mountains right outside our back door," Billie said with pride.

Nikki tossed Billie a you-have-to-be-kidding look. "I could never live in that kind of place."

"I'll bet San Francisco is a great place to live," Lauren said, hoping Nikki would share more.

Nikki's eyes lit up. "It sure is. Tons of things to do. Shows, coffeehouses, Fisherman's Wharf, shopping, trolley cars, you name it. People everywhere."

Billie chewed the last of her cinnamon roll and shook her head. "I wouldn't enjoy that at all. Give me the wide open countryside. Throw in some mountains, and I'm in heaven."

"Well, I appreciate the mountains as well as the next one, but small towns sure cut down on the available men, I can tell you." Everyone looked at Gracie. She hurried on to say, "Not that I have any problems." She gave a nervous laugh. "My goodness, no." She pressed her hand against her chest with all the drama of Scarlett O'Hara. "I just have more callers than I know what to do with," she said in her Southern drawl. At this point, Lauren could visualize a waving hankie. "Why, just the other day—"

"Then why did you come here if you've got so many callers?" Nikki asked with an edge of sarcasm.

Lauren wanted to cheer *Go, Nikki!* Instead she kept her tongue locked behind her teeth.

Gracie's eyelashes blinked in rapid succession. "Why—" dramatic pause here "—whatever do you mean by that?" she asked with the daintiest of gasps. Her bottom lip protruded in the cutest little ol' Southern way. The woman deserved an Oscar.

Nikki didn't look impressed in the least. She took another bite of toast. "Seems to me you wouldn't need this contest if you had so many guys knocking at your door."

Gracie blinked once this time. Her pout turned to a sort of snarl. Yeah, that was it, Lauren decided. Definitely a snarl. Lauren wanted to call out "Catfight!" but maturity held her in check.

"Oh, honey, it's an adventure." She stood and turned to leave the room. She stopped at the door and paused for effect. "And just in case you're all wondering, I do plan to *Win Daddy's Heart.*" As she was leaving the room, Gracie looked back at Lauren and tossed her a wicked grin, graced ever so slightly with Southern gentility.

Before anyone could react to Gracie, Garrett stepped back into the room.

They shifted their gaze from where Gracie had stood and turned to look at Garrett.

"Are you guys okay? You look as though you've just lost a major credit card." He laughed.

Billie grunted. "In our part of the country, we've got friendlier grizzlies," she mumbled, walking past a puzzled Garrett.

Nikki's lip curled before she went back to her breakfast. Ellen stared at her plate as if someone had tied her nose to it.

Lauren glanced at Garrett, wondering if he had any idea what his daughters had gotten him into.

Garrett laid his pen on the desk and rubbed his eyes. He thought he had heard Lauren talking to someone in the great room. He figured he'd earned a break from the ledgers, so he decided to get up and go check on what everybody was doing.

A spark shot through him when he stepped into the great room and saw Lauren. He liked the way her yellow top brought out the golden highlights in her hair. "Hi," he said, sauntering over to the sofa. Garrett looked around. "I thought I heard you talking with someone."

"Oh, Ellen just left. She and I were discussing a book she's reading.

He sat down beside her. "Nice pocket PC."

Lauren punched something with her stylus, watched the screen a minute, then shut it down. "Thanks," she said, looking up.

"What did we do before all the modern conveniences?" he teased.

"I'm sure I don't know. I only know I wouldn't want to be without them."

For some reason, he just didn't want to talk about that right now. "Where did everybody go?" he asked, looking around.

"Macy took the women down to the beach area to just hang out for a little while."

"Didn't you want to go?"

She shook her head. "I just needed some alone time."

"I'm sorry. I shouldn't have bothered you." Garrett started to get up.

"No, no. Don't go." The way she said that made him weak in the knees. "I just meant I didn't feel like being around a lot of people." She looked at him a moment. "I thought you were gone."

"I've been working on the B and B accounts." He rubbed the back of his neck. "Not my favorite thing to do."

She smiled. "I don't blame you there."

One look into Lauren's eyes and Garrett's teeth seemed to stick together as though he'd been eating taffy.

"You okay?" she asked with a teasing glint in her eyes.

He wanted to say, *Does the fact that you turn my insides to mush mean anything to you?* Instead, he said, "Yeah, why?"

"Oh, I don't know. You just sort of had a funny look on your face."

Susie had always told him he was transparent. She could see right through him. He'd better be more careful. "Just born that way, I guess."

They fell silent a moment.

"Hey, what was that all about at breakfast?" he asked.

Lauren chuckled. "Female stuff. You don't want to go there."

"Oh, what have my girls gotten me into?"

"Exactly." Lauren laughed again.

"Are you ready to disown your friends yet for getting you caught in this mess?"

She looked up at him. "Oh, not just yet." Amusement lifted the corners of her mouth.

"Something tells me you've got an ornery side."

"You think so?"

"I think so."

"Well, I guess you'll just have to wait and see."

Now he lifted a brow. "Is that a challenge?"

"Maybe. But you have less than two weeks to find out," she teased.

Suddenly the bantering took a serious turn for him. The thought of less than two weeks with Lauren Romey bothered him. He wondered if his feelings for her were changing. Had his daughters actually stumbled onto something with this contest? He had never entertained the thought of another woman after Susie's death. He didn't have that right. How could he go on living and enjoying life when she had lost hers?

"So having said that, I believe the little green men did come from Mars," Lauren said.

Garrett looked at her with a start, wondering what in the world she was talking about.

She laughed and picked up a cup of coffee she had placed on the stand beside her. "You see, I knew you weren't listening."

Garrett relaxed. "You're right. I'm sorry. I got side-tracked."

"By what?"

The depth of turquoise in your eyes, the curve of your lips, the way your hair glistens in the light of day. You. He mentally shook himself. Garrett, get a grip here. He blew out a breath. "I'm sorry, Lauren. Guess I just have a lot on my mind."

She nodded.

Something about her was so innocent, playful, intriguing. He couldn't put his finger on it, but he knew he definitely wanted to get to know her better.

"I found your initials carved in one of the trees when I got lost," she said, then looked as if she wished she hadn't.

He had forgotten about that tree. "It was the day we bought the house. Susie and I went into the woods and we—" Garrett stopped.

"I'm sorry, Garrett. I didn't mean to pry."

"No, it's all right. It's been three years."

"Yes, but I'm sure it's still painful."

His thoughts blasted him. He wanted to get the subject off him. "And what about you, Lauren? As pretty as you are, I'm sure you've left a trail of broken hearts."

She shrugged. "Oh, I don't know. I wanted to get my career off the ground before I thought about a serious relationship."

"And did you?"

"Well, obviously since I lost my job, I haven't gotten very far."

"So you're telling me there is no one special in your life—or am I being too forward to ask?"

Lauren paused a moment and took a deep breath.

"There was someone special." She rubbed her bare ring finger. "We were engaged."

The information surprised him, because she was here for the contest, though it surprised him more she hadn't been snatched up by someone. "I take it that fell through?"

"Yeah."

"The friend who betrayed you?"

"Good memory."

"You don't have to talk about it, if you'd rather not."

"No, it's okay." She told him what had happened.

"That's tough." He reached over and pulled her hand between both of his. "I'm really sorry."

"Thank you. But God is getting me through."

An awkward moment followed and he pulled his hand away.

"Is something wrong?"

"What? No. It's just that…"

"Garrett, what is it?"

"How can you believe in a God who lets bad things happen?" Garrett turned to Lauren. "He could have saved her. I believed He would."

"But I thought…you…"

"You thought that because I take my girls to church…" He let the words hang between them.

Lauren looked down.

"I do it for them and because that's what their mother would have wanted me to do. Once they're out of the house, I won't step foot in a church again. He wasn't there for me. I won't be there for Him."

"Just because you don't believe doesn't change who He is, Garrett."

He said nothing.

"I'm sorry you feel that way," Lauren said in barely a whisper.

"Life goes on. Not for Susie, though. He made sure of that."

Lauren rose from the sofa. "I need to go upstairs."

"You going somewhere?"

"I thought I would check out the spa in Tahoe that Macy told me about."

"Too much isolation, nature and fresh air out here for you, huh?" he asked. He could hear the irritation in his voice, but couldn't help himself. Just when he thought he could get close to this woman, she reminded him of their differences. Modern conveniences and God stood between them. She had her head in the clouds. He lived in a world of reality.

And the reality was they lived worlds apart.

Chapter Seven

Lauren grabbed the directions to the spa off her bed and stuffed it in her handbag. She had to shake off the gloom Garrett's words had brought. That's what she got for assuming he was walking with the Lord. Instead, he had let bitterness take root in his heart. She wanted to help him, but she wasn't exactly the voice of authority. She had to work through a little bitterness of her own.

Not wanting to bother Garrett and needing time to think away from him, Lauren took a cab to pick up a rental car. She was glad she had waited a few days and taken time to get acclimated to her surroundings before trying to drive.

The afternoon breeze seemed to dust Bliss Village to a vibrant sparkle. The town smelled summertime clean. Lauren paid for the rental of a white convertible and climbed into the driver's seat. Retrieving her map, she unfolded it and looked it over. Once satisfied she knew where she was going, she put on her sunglasses and eased into the traffic.

The trip was longer than she had remembered from her times with Gwen and Candace. Tahoe was a good clip from Bliss Village. Oh, well. At least there were fun things to do there. She went first to a nail salon—well, after getting lost a couple of times, that is, and finally having to ask for directions. Getting her nails done made her feel feminine and complete in her appearance. To Lauren, going into public without her nails done was akin to going to church without shoes.

Once the cherry-red polish sparkled from her fingertips, she headed for the day spa. Totally enjoying her day of pampering, she could hardly wait for a massage, hoping it would relax her. After all, that's why Gwen and Candace had sent her to Bliss Village in the first place.

A mixture of sweet-smelling perfumes and oils welcomed Lauren as she stepped into the day spa. The place was smaller than she had expected, but nice. A reception area was situated at the front of the room. A woman took her name and ushered her back into a small waiting area where candles glowed and soothing music played overhead. They served her chamomile tea. Women's self-improvement magazines fanned out on the coffee table and Lauren reached over to read through one. Before she had gotten too far into an article on the benefits of exercise, a petite young woman appeared and called her name.

They walked into a private room lit by a couple of vanilla-scented candles, with a tray of oils and perfumes nearby. The woman instructed Lauren to prepare for the massage and climb beneath the warm blanket on the bed in the middle of the room. The woman would return in a few minutes. The soothing music continued to play. Once Lauren settled onto the bed, she felt her tension begin to dissolve. With the effects from the subdued lighting, soft music and pleasing aroma, she felt her eyelids grow heavy. Why didn't she do this more often?

The woman soon entered and asked Lauren about her preferred scents. Practically in a hypnotic state, Lauren struggled to keep her speech from slurring as she answered. The woman set to work. She placed a warm cloth lightly over Lauren's eyes and started massaging the tension from her shoulders. By the time Lauren prepared to leave, she felt totally at peace with the world. She didn't think even Gracie Jane Skinner could rile her today. Lauren paid for her treatment and noticed a sign on the wall indicating that the spa also offered body wraps and mud treatments. She'd be back.

With legs that felt like cooked spaghetti, she took great care as she stepped out the door and into the bright sunlight blazing over the parking lot. She stopped at the door of her convertible and took a deep breath. The day couldn't possibly get any better—a box of chocolate truffles might do the trick, but Lauren knew she couldn't have everything. She climbed into her car and finally edged into traffic. Heading down the main road, she spotted a quaint boutique on her right and decided to check it out.

Once she was inside, a parade of colorful fabrics, scarves and hats filled her vision like eye candy. The smell of leather reached her before she came upon the handbags and matching shoes. At every turn, Lauren practically hyperventilated from sheer delight.

She thought it couldn't hurt to have something new

to wear when it was her time to go out with Garrett—after all, she'd thought this was just a relaxing vacation. She hadn't packed for a romantic outing. Who wouldn't want to look their best on a date? It had nothing to do with Garrett—or so she told herself.

Settling in for a wonderful time of shopping, Lauren browsed through the rows of suits and coordinates, trying on things here and there until she finally found the perfect outfit, a classic navy pantsuit with matching jewelry, handbag and shoes. By the time she walked out of the boutique, she felt invigorated and refreshed. Funny how shopping could do that for her. The very fact that she had no job and no possibilities in the near future didn't deter her joy in the least. Okay, maybe it nagged at her a little, but she refused to dwell on the idea. This was a great day. She would not allow little things such as unemployment, a shrinking bank account and mounting bills spoil it for her.

Why, she all but skipped her way back to the car.

As she returned to the bed-and-breakfast, Lauren thought about the different contestants, and her thoughts finally settled on Nikki Spartan. Lauren could only imagine how exciting it must feel to live in a huge metropolis such as San Francisco. Noise, people, endless events—a town that never slept. She thought of the places she'd lived. She'd grown up in a town surrounded by cornfields and cattle, where everyone went to bed at sundown and got up before the *Today Show.* She couldn't even get a signal for her cell phone in the area. Now she lived and worked in a nearby fairly good-sized city. Make that *had* worked. Still, it wasn't as hustling and bustling as San Francisco.

By the time she arrived at the inn, she had made up her mind to do an Internet search for jobs in the big city. With her parents now living in Florida, she had nothing to hold her to Indiana. The entire world was at her disposal. She could look for a job anywhere! She stepped out of the car. Her eyes took in the distant mountains beyond the inn. The words *even Bliss Village* whispered to her heart. "Yeah, right, as if I'd want to live here," she said to herself. With the exception of a few mountains thrown in here and there, Bliss Village didn't differ all that much from where she had grown up. Not that she didn't love to visit. She did. But living there—and finding employment—would be another matter entirely.

She reached into the backseat for her packages. Before her mood could take a nosedive, she decided she'd go upstairs and try on her new pantsuit.

Entering the inn, she could hear someone shuffling papers in the den. Since the girls' car was gone, she assumed it was Garrett. She had no idea where the other contestants were, but she didn't really care. She still wanted to be alone. Quietly she made her way up the stairs and slipped into her room.

Placing her bag on the bed, she pulled out the tissue and clothing items one by one. Her heart kicked up a couple of notches. She could hardly wait to try on her things. It had been a while since she'd purchased new clothes. She had on her new pantsuit in no time. Once her new jewelry was in place, she walked over to her dresser and swept her hair off her neck and onto the back of her head, pinning it in place. Her hair was too short to do anything fancy, but after she looked it over she decided the current updo would suffice.

She couldn't imagine why she was going to such great lengths, but she needed to get an idea of just how she would wear her hair when she and Garrett went out. Not that she wanted to impress him, but still, a woman wanted to look her best. This was a contest, after all, and she was just doing her part—or so she told herself.

With her hair secured in place, she adjusted her makeup—a little more blush, touch-up on her eyeliner and shadow. Finally a little more lipstick and presto, she was finished. Putting her makeup away, she took a good look at her reflection. She decided she didn't look half bad. Although she didn't know where Garrett would take her for sure, she felt pretty confident this pantsuit would do the trick, wherever they went.

Someone knocked on the door.

Oh, dear. She didn't really want the others to see her in her outfit. They would think she actually wanted to win this contest. Another knock.

"Lauren, are you in there?" Garrett's voice sounded beyond the door, causing Lauren's heart to flip.

Good grief.

She took another glance in the mirror, tucked in a stray hair and headed for the door. "Yes, I'm here. I'm coming."

Opening the door, she stood face-to-face with Garrett. "Yes?"

Garrett could feel himself staring, but he seemed completely unable to stop. It reminded him of those dreams he'd had when he was little where he showed up at school barefoot, but had no idea how to get his shoes.

A navy-blue outfit covered Lauren's slender frame.

Her complexion looked so creamy, he wanted to touch her to see if it was real. Her blond hair was pulled up on the back of her head, revealing a soft neck. She took his breath away, literally.

"Garrett?" he heard her say again.

"Yeah, uh, Lauren..." Man! He couldn't remember for the life of him what he had come to see her about. He heard her chuckle. He was making a fool of himself, and he didn't know what to do.

Nocchi barked.

That jarred him loose. "Uh, yeah, the girls made lasagna for dinner, but I'm not sure it has enough garlic. Could you taste it for me?" he asked, feeling stupid but reaching for any excuse to get him through this awkward moment. Her expression told him she could see right through him.

"Uh, sure, I'd be glad to. I just got home and wanted to try on...I mean, I bought some—well, give me a minute to change, and I'll be right down."

He couldn't hide his amusement. Seemed they both were stammering. "Sorry to bother you." He started to turn, but stopped himself short. "By the way, um, you look great." He quickly turned and went down the stairs before she could utter a word, though he felt sure he heard a gasp catch in her throat. The thought pleased him. A lot. He looked back toward her door, knowing she'd be down in a minute to check out the lasagna.

He scratched his jaw. Come to think of it, his face was feeling a little rough. Since she was going to be changing her clothes, he figured he'd have time for a quick shave before Lauren made it down. He stepped into his bathroom, shaved, splashed on a little cologne, ran a comb through his hair and adjusted the collar of his shirt. After he was satisfied with the look, he headed out.

With his mind fixed on Lauren, he practically plowed into Gracie once he entered the kitchen. Her arms stopped him and lingered on his chest. Gracie laughed. "Whoa, big boy. Where you all going in such a hurry?" She was a pretty one, all right, but something about her didn't sit quite right with Garrett.

She stood face-to-face with him, not moving an inch. "I'm sorry, Gracie." He stepped back. "I didn't mean to run into you."

She stepped forward, put her hands against his chest once more and looked into his eyes. "Why, Garrett, honey, you can run into me any ol' time you want." She took a deep breath. "Umm, you smell good."

Footsteps sounded behind them.

"Oh, excuse me," Lauren said, freezing in place.

She felt heat climb her face, and it made her angry. She wasn't doing anything to be embarrassed about, after all. That seemed to be Gracie and Garrett's department.

Garrett immediately stepped away from Gracie's grasp. An awkward moment hung between them. There was that wicked grin from Gracie again. Lauren wanted to smear it all over her face. Okay, that wasn't Christian, but right now she was struggling.

"I—I was just going to check your lasagna, but I can come back later." She turned to go.

"No, Lauren, wait." Garrett's voice pricked her heart, but she'd been down this road before.

Lauren went upstairs to her room and closed the

door behind her. Once inside she sagged onto her bed, trembling. Seeing Gracie in such an intimate moment with Garrett had brought back the pain of Jeff and Camilla. That's all it was. It's not like she and Garrett had anything going. It wasn't that she still loved Jeff—it was more a matter of revisiting the betrayal. Maybe even a pride thing. How could the two people she had cared so much about all these years do something so painful? Tears trickled down her cheeks.

My life is such a mess, God. I never dreamed it could turn out this way. I know You're in control, but sometimes it feels as though You're not. Jeff and Camilla hurt me deeply, Lord. I don't want to feel bitter about that, and I want to forgive them, but right now I just don't know how. I need You to do it through me. I have no idea how that will happen, but I just want You to know it's nothing I can do on my own. I don't have the compassion or mercy. I'm mad at them plenty for the pain they have caused me.

More tears streaked down her face while she prayed in the quiet of her room. When she had finished, she wasn't sure she had all the answers, but at least she knew she wasn't alone. She'd get through it all somehow, one step at a time.

After she washed her face and reapplied her makeup, a knock sounded at her door. She still didn't want to talk to Garrett, and she hoped it wasn't him. Reluctantly she walked over and answered the door. It was Macy.

"I'm sorry to bother you, Lauren. It's just that I overheard…I thought…I—I don't mean to intrude."

Lauren couldn't help smiling at the young woman. "You're not intruding. Come on in. I could use a little company."

Macy stepped inside Lauren's room.

"I didn't know you were home," Lauren said.

"We got home just about the time you were heading for your room. I wasn't going to bother you, but well, you seemed upset." She settled in a chair, and Lauren sat on her bed. Macy hesitated. "Are you sorry you came here?"

Her question startled Lauren. "What? No—no, of course not. It's not that at all. I just have some things I need to work through."

"I know how that is."

Lauren wasn't sure what to say. "How about you—are you doing okay?"

"Yeah." She stared at her hands in her lap. "We just wanted this to be fun for Dad. It's not quite turning out the way we had hoped."

The vision of Gracie and Garrett in the kitchen popped into Lauren's mind. "Oh I don't know, I think your dad seems to be enjoying himself."

Macy looked at her. "You think so?"

Lauren felt herself go soft toward the motherless girl who seemed to carry the weight of the world on her shoulders. "Yes, I think so. I'm sure he appreciates all that you and Molly have done for him."

Macy shook her head. "I've done a lot, all right," she said in a whisper.

"I'm sorry?"

"Nothing."

"Are you looking forward to college?" Lauren asked.

"I guess so."

Lauren chuckled. "You don't sound very convincing."

"I don't know. Nothing is the same since—"

A pang twisted in Lauren's heart. Macy was hurting deeply from her mother's death. Lauren wanted to help her, but wasn't sure how to go about it. "You miss her a lot, I'm sure."

Macy nodded as tears filled her eyes. Obviously uncomfortable with sharing so much, she lifted her chin and seemed to swallow back the tears. "Well, nothing we can do about it now," she said, as if to stop further conversation. She stood and started for the door.

"Macy?"

Macy turned to Lauren.

"I'll be praying for you."

Surprise lit her face. "Thanks, Lauren." She turned and walked out of the room.

Chapter Eight

The next night the ladies gathered around the fireplace in the great room, knowing the newsman would be there later.

"Let me get these out of the way," Molly said, removing the books from the coffee table.

"Thanks, Molly." Macy placed the tray of mugs filled with hot chocolate on the table in the space Molly had created. "Here we go," Macy said, looking rather proud of her hostessing skills.

"It looks delicious, Macy," Lauren said.

The other contestants agreed—all except one. Gracie was out on her special date with Garrett, a fact Lauren refused to dwell on. It shouldn't bother her anyway. And it didn't, really. Well, maybe a little.

Gracie just grated on Lauren's nerves. So naturally Lauren would feel uneasy thinking about Gracie and Garrett being out together. It was the competition thing, Lauren convinced herself. She didn't want Gracie to win, because Gracie was being so nasty about it all. Lauren didn't care about winning Garrett's heart, but with the challenge placed before her, she would not back down.

"Do you know, Lauren?" Billie asked.

Lauren looked up to find everyone staring at her. "Oh, I'm sorry. I think I was kind of mesmerized by the fireplace. I didn't hear your question."

"Hey, no problem," Billie said. "I do that myself sometimes, you know, just sort of phase in and out. Happens to me when I'm out hunting for elk. You have to be patient when you're hunting, you know. Some things you just can't hurry, and hunting is one of them. You sit with your heart in your throat while the animal creeps closer and closer and then finally *pow!*"

Lauren felt a slight shiver. Nikki's mouth quirked and Ellen kept her top lip in the cream of her hot chocolate. Garrett's girls blanched visibly.

"I'm vegetarian, and I can't see why people kill defenseless animals anyway," Nikki said. Lauren could visualize Nikki carrying a huge sign, Down With Hunting, while she staged a protest in front of a gun shop.

Not wanting to get into a debate about hunting, Lauren interrupted Billie just as her mouth opened but before any words came out. "What were you asking me about, Billie?"

Billie blinked. Pausing only a moment to swallow—probably the words that begged to be released—she said, "Oh, yeah. I asked if you knew when that news guy was coming."

Lauren sighed, thankful she'd been able to deter Billie and Nikki. "Didn't he say he had some dinner he had to attend, so he would be here around nine o'clock, Macy?"

Macy looked at her watch. "I think so."

Lauren held back her amusement. Not only did she figure that Macy knew he was coming at nine o'clock, but Lauren could easily imagine that Macy had been counting the hours and minutes until his arrival. It hadn't escaped her notice that Macy had paid special attention to her appearance.

"So we've got another hour," Billie said, holding her cup of hot chocolate and scooting carefully back into her seat.

The ladies settled into a pleasant discussion of their homes, former boyfriends and schooling. With amusement, Lauren watched as Macy and Molly seemed to take it all in. No doubt forming their opinions of who they wanted for their dad—if anyone at all.

"So what do you do back home, Nikki?" Lauren asked, taking the last drink from her mug.

Nikki brightened. "I buy and sell vintage clothing on the Internet."

"Really? How interesting." Molly joined in.

"It's a trip. I love it."

The more Lauren got to know Nikki, the more impressed she was with the young woman. Nikki had a knack for business. Lauren could tell that just by listening to her. Just goes to show you can't judge a book by its cover, she thought.

"How about you, Billie?" Macy asked.

"You mean what do I do back home?"

"Uh-huh."

"You probably can't tell, but I work at a fitness center."

Was she kidding? Of course they could tell. The woman resembled a bear. Well, minus the hair and pointy teeth. Strong, intimidating. Still, Lauren could tell Billie's rough exterior covered a soft heart.

Ellen told them she worked as a librarian assistant. Lauren had no problem imagining that.

Finally everyone looked at Lauren. She squirmed a little on her seat. "Um, I was an attorney, but I lost my job before coming here."

"Oh, that's too bad," Billie said.

"Bummer," Nikki added.

"Sorry, Lauren," Macy and Molly said in unison.

"Hey, the world is a big place. I'll find something else." She grinned. "Besides, I'm kind of looking forward to totally being open to anywhere. I don't have to stay in Indiana."

"Yeah, you could always work in Bliss Village," Billie teased.

Before Lauren could respond, the doorbell rang. "He's early," Macy said with a grin, already making her way to the door.

Molly shared a glance with Lauren.

"Yes, come on in. They're in here," Macy said as she entered the room with Drew Huntington.

The young reporter was dressed in casual jeans and a preppy blue T-shirt. His short brown hair spiked upward and with one look at Macy, his dark eyes shined. In his right hand he held a small notebook and pen.

"Hey, ladies," he said with a lopsided boyish grin.

Everyone greeted him.

"In case you're wondering, one of the contestants is gone," Billie said. "She's out with the main squeeze." She winked.

"Oh." Drew stuffed his hand into his pocket.

"Can I get you anything to drink?" Macy asked the young reporter.

"No, thanks. I'll just sit down here and get to know these nice ladies," he said.

For some reason, Lauren thought his comment made them all sound matronly.

"So tell me about yourself, uh—"

"Nikki," she answered with a dry expression that said she wanted to get this whole thing over.

"Right. Sorry I don't have your names down yet."

"Not much to tell. I'm from San Francisco."

"Yes, and she's vegetarian," Billie interrupted with a grunt of disapproval.

Nikki's chin tipped upward.

Lauren figured they were in for a long night.

"And she buys and sells vintage clothing," Macy added.

"Great." Drew wrote down some notes. "How about I do it this way—I'll ask a general question, and you can each answer. Let's see, Macy and Molly have filled me in on how they got the word out on the Internet about this contest. What made you want to sign up?"

Nikki jumped in first. "I was bored. I haven't been to Bliss Village or the Lake Tahoe area since I was kid. That was back when my parents were still married. And let's see, they're both on partner number four, so it's been a while."

"Well, me and Dirk the Jerk broke up, so I figured I'd let him know I wasn't waiting around on him," Billie said. "My biological clock is ticking, you know." She snapped her fingers in rapid succession. "It's time to take care of business," she said without the slightest hint of embarrassment.

Macy's and Molly's jaws dropped, and Lauren tried not to laugh.

Drew looked at Ellen. Everyone turned to her. In the silence she turned three shades of red. "Um, I needed a vacation. My family made me come."

Lauren thought that if Ellen ducked her head any farther into her top, she would resemble the headless horseman.

"How about you?" Drew asked, turning to Lauren, catching her off guard.

"Me?"

"Yeah, you."

"Well, actually—" She stalled for time. She wasn't sure she should explain to them that it was all a mistake. On the other hand, she couldn't lie about it.

"Oh, honey, that's easy. She's on the rebound." Gracie's voice dripped sugar from the doorway. Lauren could almost see a parasol twirling behind Gracie's little ol' head.

With the sound of a car engine outside, Lauren figured Garrett was parking the car.

"Rebound?" Drew asked, writing furiously. "Tell me more."

"There's nothing to tell," Lauren said with finality.

"Oh, that's no fun," Drew teased.

"How about I take the hot chocolate mugs and get us some popcorn and soft drinks?" Macy suggested, steering the conversation in a different direction. Lauren nodded her thanks.

Drew picked things right back up. "So are you ladies saying you didn't come here to 'Win Daddy's Heart'?"

Nikki shook her head. "Well, Garrett's a nice man and all, but I don't need a man to be complete. In fact, the men in my life have done nothing but hurt me."

Drew scooted in closer. "Oh?"

Nikki held up her hand. "Nope. That's all you're getting from me. I figured I could come here, have a good time, and if something came of it, I could live with that. If not, I can live with that, too."

Drew kept writing. "Sounds fair enough," he said when he finally looked up. He glanced around the room. "Anyone else?"

"Well, I want to say something," Gracie said as she waltzed across the floor.

Lauren half expected Fred Astaire to slip from the shadows and glide across the floor with her.

Gracie sat down, the very essence of elegance. "When I saw the announcement on the contest and got a look at Garrett's picture, honey, wild horses couldn't have kept me away." She plumped a pillow and put it on her lap.

Drew brightened. "So you want to win," he said, more as if stating a fact than asking.

"Oh, I don't just *want* to win. I am *going* to win. After my evening with Garrett tonight, I have no doubt." She fixed her gaze on Lauren.

Lauren bristled. There was that challenge again.

"If you had such a great evening, what are you doing home at nine-thirty?" Nikki asked.

Woohoo! Go, Nikki!

Gracie shifted nervously on her chair. "Oh, the poor man had a bad headache."

"Well, now, that's a surprise," Nikki mumbled.

"Excuse me?" Gracie pinned Nikki with a stare.

"I said that was wise."

Silence.

"To come home, I mean." Pause. "Since he has a headache."

"Oh, don't you worry, honey, we had a great time. And there will be more times to come." Gracie turned away and Nikki grinned at Lauren.

Drew, obviously enjoying the tension in the air, swiveled around to face Lauren. "And do you have hopes of winning?"

She heard the front door open, footsteps, then Garrett stood at the room entrance. "Hi, all," he said with a wave and a wide grin.

Lauren mentally sighed. Garrett to the rescue. She thought he looked pretty good. Too bad about the headache. She figured he would probably go right on up to bed.

"Hey, Garrett," Drew said, getting up to shake Garrett's hand. "Sorry about your headache, dude."

For an instant Garrett looked surprised. "Oh, yeah, thanks," he finally said. He glanced at Gracie, cleared his throat, then looked away. How curious.

Drew settled back into his seat and Garrett grabbed a desk chair and pulled it up beside Lauren. She didn't dare glance Gracie's way. She hoped with everything in her that Drew would not pick up where he had left off.

Drew rubbed his hands together. "Now, where was I?"

"Hold on, before you get into a deep discussion,

here's the popcorn and drinks," Macy said while she and Molly carried in the refreshments.

Macy saves the day once again, Lauren thought. Must run in the family. Lauren let out an audible sigh, causing Garrett to look at her.

"You okay?" he asked, genuine concern in his eyes.

"I'm fine. How about you?"

He cast a quick glance at Gracie and gave a slight cough. "I'm feeling a little better."

The girls passed out the popcorn and drinks. "Um, I think we were talking about why you all came to this contest," Drew said, thumbing through his notes. "Let's see, I have your hometowns, pertinent information." He looked up at Lauren. "You're not going to tell me about your rebound thing?"

Lauren shook her head. However, she did explain how her friends signed her up for the contest.

The small group sat in the room eating their snacks and enjoying comfortable fellowship. Drew gleaned a little more information, but nothing really exciting. He spent time talking with Macy then said his goodbyes and headed outside with Macy close by. Lauren stayed and talked to the ladies a little while, then went to her room. Just as she started to close her blinds, she glanced outside. When she saw Gracie talking alone with Drew, her stomach knotted. She knew that couldn't be good. She twisted the blinds closed. Oh, well, what did it matter? It wasn't as though anyone cared if she had been engaged. Garrett already knew anyway. She couldn't imagine what Gracie had hoped to gain with her disclosure of Lauren's past.

"Come on, Nocchi," she said, scooping her dog into her arms. "I need to take you outside before we call it a night."

Once Lauren arrived back in the room with Nocchi, she remembered a magazine in the great room that she had wanted to read. She decided to slip downstairs to bring it up to her room so she could read it before bed.

She sat down on the sofa a moment and browsed through the magazines.

"Mind if I join you?" Garrett's voice ran through her like warm mocha, sending up a warning flag. Remembering their differences, she steeled herself against his charm.

"No problem," she said.

He sat beside her on the sofa. "So did you have a good time at the spa?"

"It was fabulous," Lauren said. "Just what I needed." His nearness made her a little uncomfortable.

"A walk in the woods won't do it, huh?"

"I get lost in the woods, remember?"

"Oh, right," he said. A pause stood between them.

Lauren shuffled through the magazines once more. "I saw a magazine down here I wanted to read before bed," she said by way of explanation.

"I want to apologize about the way I came across this morning," he all but blurted out, as if he had been waiting all afternoon to say it.

Lauren looked up in surprise.

"About God and all. I mean, I still feel that way, but I didn't mean to come across so harsh. It's something I have to work through."

"I know all about that."

"You do?"

"I mean the working through part. I have some things to work through myself."

"The breakup?"

"Yeah."

Another pause. "Well, there is no better place to work through a problem than Bliss Village, I always say," he said with a slight grin.

"Is that right?"

"Yep. Lake Tahoe nearby for the city slickers, and the blessed pines for country folk such as me." He grinned again, but this time he watched her closely.

Lauren wondered if his comment held a hidden meaning.

He laughed. "Don't try to figure it out, just enjoy."

To her surprise and frustration, she did enjoy his nearness, the smell of his cologne, the way he looked at her. Yes, she enjoyed Garrett Cantrell, all right.

Far more than she wanted to enjoy him.

Chapter Nine

With a sigh Garrett sank onto his bed, thankful for the end to this long evening. Had he really endured only four days of this nightmare so far? His daughters owed him big-time come Father's Day. He was thinking a new bass boat just might do the trick.

He had never met a woman in all his life who could talk as much as Gracie Skinner. In fact, she barely paused to breathe. Downright alien. He could almost imagine her with pointy ears. Maybe he should check that out just in case. One could never be too careful.

Maybe he'd been watching too much sci fi lately, but still. How could any man live with that day in and day out? No wonder the woman had never married. No sane man could handle it, unless of course he were deaf.

Garrett punched his pillow a couple of times and flopped back into place. Maybe he was being too harsh, but he could not handle extended periods of time with Gracie. His head throbbed even now with the thought of it all. He'd tried to have a good time, he really had. But all that chatter. Constant talk about her beauty pageant days, endless accolades, line of suitors. The whole evening had made his head spin. Restless, he turned onto his left side and rearranged his pillow again. Tonight he'd probably dream about giant moving lips.

A slight jab pierced his consciousness. He ignored it. No doubt she meant well, and she definitely fell into the beautiful category, but Garrett could not see himself falling for Gracie. At least, not in a romantic way. Something about her just didn't mesh with him. She had made it quite obvious she was marriage material and all too eager to take the job. How could she do that when she hardly knew him?

Maybe he wasn't being fair. After all, as Gracie had droned on and on about her achievements, Garrett's mind had drifted to Lauren Romey. And he had only just met her a few days ago.

That's what puzzled him. Why did he keep thinking about Lauren when they were so wrong for each other? She loved big-city life, he did not. She believed in the God who had let him down. He glanced at the stand across from his bed and noticed the Bible. Why did he keep it there? He hadn't used it since Susie's death. Hadn't even taken it to church with him.

With a quick yank of the covers, Garrett got out of bed, walked over to the stand and picked up the Bible. He went to the wastebasket and held the Bible just over it for a full minute. Then he turned, plopped onto his knees and pulled a box from under his bed. Lifting the lid, he plunked the Bible inside, replaced the lid and shoved the whole thing back under the bed.

He brushed his hands together. "There, that should take care of that."

He didn't want to analyze what had just happened and why he couldn't throw the book away. Garrett figured he'd done enough thinking for the day.

Easing into place, he pulled the covers over his head, hoping all the while he could escape the nightmare of giant lips.

At the risk of looking a little geeky, Lauren sat down in the coffee shop, mocha in one hand and her pocket PC in the other. She hadn't played solitaire for a long time, and she decided that might be a nice change of pace right about now. She didn't know anyone in the coffee shop, probably would never see these people again this side of heaven, so why not risk a geek moment?

The B and B was beginning to get a little crowded, to her way of thinking. Lauren needed to get away. Gracie was growling more than usual, Billie didn't back down in the least, Nikki continued to have her usual edge, while Ellen was holed up in her room most of the time. Garrett seemed oblivious to it all. Molly kept busy with her friends; Macy seemed quite smitten with Drew Huntington and put out with her dad.

Lauren looked around the shop and decided this was a good getaway place. No sooner had her PC fused to life than Macy Cantrell came into the shop, looking a little forlorn. Undoubtedly, another rift between her and Garrett. Lauren didn't know what was going on between the two of them, but she could see the growing wall and wished she could help them in some way. Of course, it was none of her business and she'd best leave it alone.

Just then Macy looked over, and Lauren waved. Macy brightened and waved back. In a moment of indecision Lauren wondered if Macy would rather be alone or if she could use some company. She waited for Macy to get her drink. Afterward Macy walked her way.

"You're welcome to join me if you don't mind some company," Lauren said, shutting off her PC.

"Thanks." Macy slid into a chair across the wooden table from Lauren. "You have a pocket PC?" The young woman looked very impressed.

"I bought it back when I had an income."

"I admire you," Macy said before taking a drink from her cup.

The comment startled her.

Macy laughed. "Well, you're progressive." Her happy expression faded. "Something my dad would know nothing about."

Uh-oh. Lauren wasn't sure she wanted to be caught in the middle of this father-daughter problem. "I don't know about progressive, but I do enjoy the latest gadgets."

"That's really cool." She thought a moment. "I'm the same way, really. I love my computer, and thanks to Dad being a worrywart, he agreed to get me and Molly each a cell phone." She waited. "It's just that he stays holed up at the B and B."

Lauren looked at her, wondering how to respond. "That's why you and Molly set this contest up, to try to help him get out of his rut, so to speak?"

"Kind of." Her eyes glazed over. "Things are so different than they used to be. If only—" She started to say more, but then her eyes refocused and she stopped herself. "I don't know what's getting into me, all this talk. Believe it or not, I normally keep pretty much to myself."

"Hmm, same as your dad?"

Macy looked up. "Touché. I guess we both want to hibernate."

Since they were being honest with one another, Lauren decided to venture out a little further. "So do I detect some sparks between you and Drew Huntington?"

"Am I that obvious?"

"Probably just to me."

"He's really nice." Macy ran her fingers along a rut in the table.

"He does appear to be a nice guy. Cute, too," Lauren said before taking a drink of her coffee.

Macy's wide eyes looked at Lauren. "Do you think so?"

"Sure." Lauren put her cup on the table.

Her right eye twitched a couple of times. "I don't think Dad cares for him all that much."

"Why?"

"Who knows? Dad doesn't seem to like much of anything these days." Macy stared into the distance. "I have a scholarship for college. Dad is afraid if I get interested in someone, I'll lose my scholarship and mess up my future. But I'm not stupid. I wouldn't throw everything away. I just want to enjoy a friendship."

"I'm sure your dad would understand if you tried talking to him about it."

"I really think it's more than that, so I just don't say much."

"How do you mean?" Lauren asked, finishing the last drop of her coffee.

"It doesn't matter," Macy said. She put on a bright expression and quickly changed the subject. "So, are you having fun here?"

"It's been really interesting," Lauren said with a chuckle.

"I hope everyone doesn't think it's a total bust." Worry lines formed between Macy's brows.

"I don't think so at all, Macy. I think it's really sweet that you and Molly have done this for your dad. It's a nice treat for all the ladies. We get to see the beautiful scenery, stay in a lovely bed-and-breakfast. Not to mention the fact that your dad is quite a catch," she said, trying to make Macy feel better.

Macy perked up. "Do you think so?"

Lauren swallowed hard. Of course she did think so, but she didn't really want to encourage Macy all that much. Lauren needed time to heal from her last serious relationship. Besides, it wasn't as though Garrett was all that attracted to her. She knew he enjoyed her company in a friendly sort of way, but she felt sure it ended there. He was undoubtedly still in love with his deceased wife.

"Well?" Macy asked, her gaze still on Lauren.

"Well, yeah, I think he's a very nice guy."

Macy sat back. "I'm glad you think so, Lauren."

The look on Macy's face made Lauren feel a little uncomfortable. Did Macy think her troubles would all be over if her dad found a woman?

"Well, I'd better get back to the B and B," Macy said. "I just needed a little break from Gracie's constant chatter—" She covered her mouth with her hand.

Lauren looked toward the ceiling and whistled as if she hadn't heard a thing.

"I shouldn't have said that."

"It's okay. I understand." They both threw away their cups and talked about the nice weather on the way to their cars. Lauren settled into her seat and snapped on her seatbelt. She thought of Macy's comment about Gracie and smiled. She liked Macy Cantrell. She liked her a lot.

Lauren spent the afternoon at a neighborhood park, reading a novel she had picked up earlier in the day. The park overlooked Lake Tahoe. A gentle wind kept the sun's heat at bay, making for a wonderfully relaxing day. She hadn't wanted to show up at the B and B this morning right after coffee. If she and Macy had arrived at the same time, it would only have fueled Gracie's snide comments. Gracie seemed to think Lauren had ulterior motives about everything.

By the time Lauren entered the B and B, Macy was sitting alone in the great room.

"Hey, Macy," Lauren said.

"Hi."

"Where is everybody?"

"Dad took Nikki and Billie to the store to pick up some things they needed. Gracie is resting in her room." She leaned toward Lauren. "Hopefully, she'll stay there a while," she added in a whisper, holding up her hands with crossed fingers.

Lauren winked.

"And Molly is at a friend's house."

"So you're just enjoying your free time while everyone's out, huh?"

"Well, I was getting ready to start some dinner. Thought we'd have spaghetti, salad and garlic bread tonight. In case you haven't noticed, we like pasta."

"Sounds good to me."

Before they could talk further, someone knocked at the front door. Macy went to answer it.

"Drew, hi!"

Lauren could see why Macy was attracted to the reporter, with his deep dimples that complemented a wide smile and sharp preppy clothes. Lauren smiled a greeting, then walked into the kitchen to get a drink of water so they could be alone. After filling her glass, she looked around the kitchen. She wouldn't have thought a rustic/cottage decor would have appealed to her, but she had to admit there was a certain charm about it. Too bad the place was so far from big-city life. Still, she had to admit she enjoyed the visit to Bliss Village each time she came with Gwen and Candace. She finished her water, which tasted good and cold. Placing the glass in the sink, she walked around the corner and overheard Macy talking to Drew.

"I really want to come, Drew. I do. It's just that I'm in charge of dinner for the ladies tonight. Dad would have my hide." She tried to laugh, but Lauren could hear the disappointment in Macy's voice.

"I can do it," Lauren interrupted, without giving it another thought.

Macy turned to her. A huge grin spread across Drew's face.

"What?" Macy asked.

"I said I can do it," Lauren said, smiling. "In fact, I know a great recipe for stuffed pasta shells that is simply delicious. Would it be all right if I prepared that instead? We could still have the garlic bread, salad, all the fixings, but substitute the shells for the spaghetti?"

Macy stared in disbelief. "You'd do that for me?"

"Well, of course I would. I'd be happy to. I rarely cook and it might be fun."

The beginnings of a grin teased the corners of Macy's lips.

Macy turned back to Drew. "Well, I guess I can go."

"Great!" His eyes sparkled. "You might want to take a sweater, since it gets cold around the lake in the evening."

Macy turned back to Lauren. "We're going to hear a band perform at the park. Thank you so much, Lauren. I owe you one."

It felt good to Lauren to help a couple of kids have a fun evening together. "No problem. Glad to help."

In the blink of an eye, Macy and Drew were out the door. Lauren went up to her room to get her purse so she could rush to the store and buy what she needed for dinner.

It took her no time at all to get the ingredients and return in time to prepare their dinner. Placing everything on the counter, she set to work.

"Well, well, well. Don't you appear to be the busy little housewife today," Gracie said.

Lauren turned with a start. Gracie's eyes narrowed. Lauren refused to be intimidated by her. "I'm just helping with dinner, Gracie."

Gracie's eyebrows rose. "Oh, and I wonder how Garrett will feel about you covering for Macy." She smiled. "Yes, I heard your conversation and saw them leave together."

Lauren wasn't sure what to make of that. Would it be a problem? Oh, sure, Macy had suggested her dad didn't want her in a relationship, but surely he wouldn't object to a casual friendship.

"Oh, you didn't know? The other night I heard them arguing in the den. They had quite a battle over this reporter guy." Gracie looked all too happy that Lauren might have to face the heat.

"Well, there's not much I can do about it now," Lauren said with more confidence than she felt.

Just then the back door swished open. Garrett, Nikki and Billie entered.

"Somebody's in trouble," Gracie said in a singsong voice as she walked past Lauren toward Garrett. "Well, hello. We're glad you're back."

"We were only gone a little while, Gracie," Garrett said, sounding a little irritated.

"Well, we still missed you," she said, her voice sickeningly sweet.

Lauren kept busy in the kitchen. The pasta shells were boiling on the stove while she blended the filling for them.

"Wow, what's all this?" Garrett asked, obviously pleased with what he saw. "You helping Macy tonight?"

Lauren exchanged a glance with Gracie, who stood with a cocky expression on her face.

"Well, uh—" Lauren didn't normally stammer, but in light of what Gracie had said, Lauren wasn't sure how to respond.

Garrett stared at her. "Macy is helping, isn't she?"

Lauren stood before him speechless.

"Well, no," Gracie said, feigning innocence. "She went out with that reporter guy. Oh, my, he is just too cute. What girl wouldn't flip head over heels for him?" She put her hand dramatically against her chest. "Isn't that right, Lauren?" Without waiting for an answer, she added, "And Lauren honey told Macy she would be all too happy to get dinner for us. Wasn't that just the sweetest thing for her to do?"

Gracie batted her little ol' eyelashes and Lauren wanted to rip them out one by one. Someone could use a little anger management here, she told herself.

It didn't help.

"Lauren, might I have a word with you in the den, please?" Garrett said through clenched teeth. "Gracie, please keep an eye on whatever is boiling in the pot."

The room grew quiet. Lauren placed her mixing spoon on the counter, wiped her hands on a nearby checkered towel and followed Garrett like a kid going to the principal's office. A nervous knot grew in her stomach with every step.

Once inside the den, Garrett closed the door behind them.

"Garrett, I'm sorry if I—"

He held up his hand. "I don't blame you, Lauren. You couldn't have possibly known that this was not a good thing. Macy took advantage of you, and that makes me angry. I'm sorry you were caught in the middle. You couldn't have known how I feel about Macy forming a relationship when she is so close to starting college—"

This time Lauren held up a hand. "Yes, I did."

He stopped abruptly. "What did you say?"

She swallowed. "I said I did know."

"But how could you know?"

She examined her fingers "Macy told me."

He stepped closer to her. "When did Macy tell you? Why did she tell you? And why would you encourage her if you knew how I felt about it?" His voice rose with every question.

"Well, first of all, she came to the coffee shop today while I was there. She sat down at my table. We talked. She mentioned she enjoyed Drew's company but that you didn't want him around. I asked her why and she said something about having a scholarship and you didn't want her to mess that up with a boyfriend relationship."

Garrett frowned at her.

"She also said she didn't want that kind of a relationship with a guy—she just wanted to enjoy a friendship. That was it."

Garrett opened his mouth.

"Oh, wait. She also said something about she thought it was more than that. But then she quickly changed the subject as if she didn't want to talk about it."

Garrett began to pace. "Let me get this straight. She told you how I felt about her having a relationship with a boy, but still you took it upon yourself to offer to cover dinner for her so she could go out?" He stopped directly in front of Lauren. "Where did she go, by the way?" The frown persisted, his face mere inches from her.

She bristled. Where did he get off treating her as a child? She was a grown woman and would not stand for it from him or any other man. For Macy's sake, Lauren attempted to stay calm. She didn't want to get

Macy into any more trouble than she was in already. "She went to the park to listen to a band."

He ran a hand through his hair and started pacing again.

"Listen, Garrett, she's not a child…."

He stopped and turned to her again. "No, you listen. Macy is not *your* daughter. You had no right whatsoever to interfere."

"I didn't realize I was interfering. I really didn't think you would mind."

"You didn't think is right," he snapped. He cocked his head to one side. "You have no idea what's going on between me and my daughter."

"I can see that she's hurting and you refuse to console her," Lauren blurted out before she could stop herself.

His face registered the shock that she felt.

"You know nothing about it, Lauren. And I will thank you to stay out of our affairs."

"Fine."

"Fine."

"Now, if you're finished with your little speech, I need to see to dinner." With that, Lauren turned on her heels and marched out the door.

Chapter Ten

Dispiritedly Garrett fell into his chair in the den. Macy had purposely defied him. And she had dragged Lauren into it. Lauren should have known better. She had a lot to learn before she had her own kids. He leaned his head back on the chair and stared at the ceiling.

Maybe he was overreacting. After all, Macy wasn't engaged or in a serious relationship. Just two kids on a date—wasn't that how Lauren had put it?

Susie would have known how to handle the matter. But Susie was not there. She would never be there again. With a heart growing cold, Garrett lifted his eyes heavenward. "You've seen to that."

Deep down he knew it wasn't God's fault, though he didn't want to admit to the truth. Garrett had failed to get the tire changed. If he had done his part, Susie would still be with him. It wasn't God's fault Garrett had failed to do his job. But God could have fixed it. That's what Garrett couldn't get past. He believed God was all-powerful. So why hadn't He done something to help Susie? Instead, He'd done nothing and now Garrett raised his two daughters alone.

A knock sounded at the door. "Garrett, honey, dinner is ready," Gracie called.

"I'll be right there."

He heard her footsteps retreat down the hallway. The last thing he needed was to endure more of her constant chatter. With a deep sigh he heaved himself out of his chair and walked out of the den to join the others for dinner.

Upon entering the dining room, he noticed the candles on the table and the nice plates. His gaze turned to Lauren. Her set jaw and narrow eyes told him he'd better not push her anymore tonight or she'd give him what for. He turned away.

Everyone settled around the table.

"This smells awesome, Lauren," Nikki said.

Billie grunted. "I'm not surprised you'd think so, since you're a vegetarian." She rolled her eyes, then quickly turned to Lauren. "Not that it doesn't smell good, Lauren. And I'm sure it's delicious. I'm just used to having a slab of beef on my plate."

"I understand," Lauren said with a slight grin.

Once they were seated, Garrett scooped a bite of pasta and sauce on his fork and raised it to his mouth.

"If you don't mind, may I offer grace?" Lauren asked.

A snicker or two sounded around the table as Garrett placed his fork back on the plate.

"Father, we thank You for this meal, for Your constant mercy and grace. We thank You for this family and ask that You would bless Garrett, Macy and Molly in the days ahead and fill their home with Your presence so that everyone who enters in will see Your love through them. Amen."

It took a moment for anyone to move. Garrett realized everyone was waiting for him, but he had been struck by Lauren's simple prayer. She had actually asked God to bless their home and those who would enter. He had never really thought of making their bed-and-breakfast such a place as that. But of course, he wouldn't think about that. He and God weren't exactly on speaking terms.

Much to Gracie's obvious dismay, the meal was a huge success. Afterward, everyone left the table and went to the great room, where they could relax with pie and coffee. Lauren helped Garrett in the kitchen with the coffee and dessert.

"Listen, Lauren, I didn't mean to come across so harsh. It's just that—"

"Garrett, you made your point. I'm not a little child you have to keep going over the lesson with. I thought I was helping, but obviously you felt I was intruding. It won't happen again." She turned and walked out carrying the dessert tray. She was in no mood to discuss it, so he let it go.

Once they were all seated in the great room and the dessert and coffee had been served, Garrett made an announcement. "The weatherman reports tomorrow will be warm and sunny. So I've decided we can all take a hike through alpine country." He practically rocked on his heels, thinking they would go along with the idea.

He was wrong.

A few gasps went up, Gracie dropped her fork, Nikki grunted and Ellen's glasses slid down her nose.

Billie was the only one smiling. "Sounds good to me," she said, caught up in the excitement of it all. He thought for a moment she might get up and whack him on the back.

"It's a little different going hiking in the Lake Tahoe area," he explained. "You'll need sturdy hiking boots, not sneakers or sandals. You'll be walking over sharp granite that can cut into thin-soled shoes. If you don't have hiking boots with you, we have quite a few different sizes that we keep on hand for our guests. I'll let you go through those."

"Is this a required activity?" Gracie wanted to know.

"Well, you're grown women, Gracie. No one has to go if they don't want to. But I would appreciate it if everyone went." He made sure his tone let her know he wanted them to go. With a frown she shifted on her seat. Good, she got his message loud and clear.

"You'll need to wear thick hiking socks and bring a spare set along. We'll douse our feet with talcum powder before we go. I'll have plenty of bandages for blisters."

"Sounds wonderful," Gracie grumbled.

"You'll need a day pack with twin water bottles. We have plenty of those things on hand too, so I'll see that you get what you need."

Billie resembled a hunter going in for the kill.

"Though nice weather is predicted, Tahoe is known for afternoon thundershowers. So we'll need to take some rain gear. We have fold-up ponchos available. I'll take flashlights and matches in case we're there past dark."

Ellen choked.

"You okay, Ellen?"

She put a hand to her throat and nodded.

"We'll be taking a moderately strenuous trail. You all appear to be able to handle that. Does anyone have an objection?"

The women exchanged glances, but no one said anything.

"This particular trail is between two and a half and three and a half miles one way. I'll have Macy and Molly waiting at the other end to pick us up. Should only take us about four hours. I think you ladies can handle it. I don't plan on being there past dark, but hikers always need to take the necessary precautions. You need to bring extra layers of clothes, long pants, sweatshirt, that kind of thing. Temperatures can change radically between six and nine thousand feet, especially if we're climbing a peak. I'll have the girls pack us all a lunch."

The room was completely quiet.

"Do you have any questions?"

Gracie raised her hand.

"Gracie?"

"You sure we have to go? I'm not experienced in hiking, Garrett. Why, I don't know what I'll do," she said in a voice of feminine desperation.

He took a deep breath. He had one nerve left and this woman was getting on it. "You'll do fine. I won't take you on anything too severe, Gracie." He shrugged. "But of course, if you would rather not go, you can stay at the house alone."

Gracie glanced at the others, lifted her chin, then looked back at Garrett. "No, I'm sure I'll be fine."

Garrett scanned the room. "Anyone else have any questions?"

He noticed Lauren kept perfectly still. "Okay, if there are no questions, we'll plan on leaving at seven o'clock tomorrow morning."

"Seven o'clock?" Gracie whined.

"Yes, Gracie, seven o'clock. If we get too late a start, it will get hot and you'll regret it, believe me."

No one said anything.

"Great." Garrett rubbed his hands together. "I'll look forward to it." He stood to collect the dishes. Putting a few on the tray, he turned to Lauren. "Did Macy say when she would return?"

Lauren visibly stiffened. "She didn't say. I assumed she had an established curfew, and I didn't feel it my place to tell her when to come home."

He wanted to say it was not her place to let Macy go, but he couldn't blame it all on Lauren. He and Macy had problems long before tonight.

Lauren held her tongue and walked toward the stairway. Garrett caught Gracie's glance at Lauren. He half expected her to break out into a little victory dance. When Gracie saw Garrett gazing her way, her expression changed to the very essence of innocence.

Garrett glared at her, took the dessert tray and stomped off to the kitchen.

Lauren tossed and turned on her bed. Finally she sat up and glanced at the clock. Eleven. She'd heard a car arrive some time ago and assumed it was Macy returning. Could have been Molly, though.

They all had an early morning ahead of them, but she could not get to sleep. Giving up, Lauren finally pulled off the covers and got out of bed. Putting on her slippers and robe, she decided to try a cup of decaf tea. The Cantrells kept a selection out for their guests, so Lauren decided she would go down and help herself.

A couple of stairs creaked as she stepped down in the quiet of the house. Once at the bottom, she heard some murmuring. She stood perfectly still for a moment. The voices came from the den. She stepped a little closer.

"I don't know what you were thinking, Macy, to bring a complete stranger into this."

"Dad, she's not a complete stranger—and she offered," Macy's voice answered.

"She had no right."

"She was being nice. Besides, I did nothing wrong. I'm not a child. I'm nineteen." Her voice took a stubborn turn.

"You're still living under my roof—"

"Not for long."

"If your mother were here—"

"But she's not, is she, Dad? Go ahead and say it. I know what you're thinking—we both know, so you might as well say it!" Macy's voice quivered.

"Say what?" He sounded totally oblivious.

Lauren felt the conversation was taking an intimate turn. She sensed something important was about to be said and she had no right knowing it. She tiptoed away from the hallway and into the kitchen. Filling the teakettle with water at the tap, she walked it over to the stove and turned on the heat. Gathering a cup, saucer and tea bag, she slipped into a chair and waited patiently for the water to get hot.

A door opened. "Macy Cantrell, you get yourself back here," Garrett said. Footsteps. Closed door.

Lauren's heart sank. She felt responsible for the trouble between Garrett and his daughter, though she knew it went much deeper than the disagreement tonight. He needed to get things cleared up before Macy went off to college. But how? Lauren wished she could help, but she had interfered enough. Garrett had told her so. She needed to mind her own business. Besides, she was there to relax. Though she had to admit that this whole business sure got the focus off her own problems. Not exactly the way she had in mind, but still it worked.

Caught up in her thoughts, she didn't hear the approaching footsteps.

"I'm sorry, Lauren."

Glancing up, Lauren saw Macy standing in the doorway. Without another thought, Lauren stood and walked over to her. She pulled Macy into a motherly embrace. "Oh, honey, it's all right. I'm so sorry if I got you into trouble."

Macy returned the hug and started crying, really crying. Lauren suspected those tears represented a whole lot more than just the problem with her dad tonight. Lauren stood there holding her, stroking her hair, not knowing exactly what to say or do to help. "It's all right, Macy. You'll get through this."

They stood in silence for a while before Macy finally calmed down. "Do you want to talk about it?" Lauren asked.

Macy shook her head. "I can't. Not yet." She lifted her gaze to Lauren. "But thank you, Lauren. I haven't been able to talk to anyone the way I've talked with you. Well, except for—Mom."

"I understand. Just know that you can talk to

me anytime." Lauren pushed a strand of hair from Macy's face.

Macy squeezed Lauren once more, turned to leave the room, then glanced once more at her. "Oh, Lauren?"

"Yes?"

"Keep praying for me, okay?"

"I will, Macy. I promise."

Garrett stepped into the shadows of the room as Macy released Lauren and headed toward the stairway. How could his own daughter relate to a stranger but couldn't even talk to him?

He heard her footsteps retreat to her room as visions of Macy in happier times played across his mind. They had always been so close before the tragedy that took Susie. Now he didn't know how to reach his own daughter. She seemed so distant. At times he felt as though he didn't know this woman/child who masquer-aded as his firstborn.

"Oh!" Lauren said, holding her hand to her throat. "I didn't know you were there."

Garrett was caught snooping, red-handed. "I, uh, well, I was searching, uh—" He groped for an excuse while Lauren studied him. From the expression on her face, he knew she wasn't buying it.

"Do you want some tea? I was just going to make some." she said, taking him totally off guard.

"You wouldn't mind if I joined you?" he asked, feeling ever so grateful for her company right now.

"No, I wouldn't mind." She led the way into the kitchen, put two tea bags into a pot, then poured in the boiling water and set the teapot aside. She retrieved another cup from the counter where they kept them for the guests, added sugar and milk to a tray, then put it on the table in front of Garrett. She sat across from him while waiting for the tea to steep.

Garrett hung his head.

Lauren reached over and put her hand on top of his. Her touch was warm and soft…comforting.

"I'm sorry about this whole thing, Garrett. I was wrong to interfere. I had no idea—"

"It's not about that, really, Lauren. It's so much more. We've not been the same since her mother died. But what can I do? I can't change what's happened."

"No, but you can change the future," she encouraged.

He had no clue how to fix things. Too tired to think, and weary of trying to figure it all out, he rested his forehead against the palm of his hand. "How?" He could hear the hopelessness and pain mingled in his own voice.

"One step at a time."

"You make it sound so easy."

"No, I'm not implying that it's easy, Garrett. I don't mean to make light of it. I know Macy loves you. I don't know what the problem is either, but she knows. She's just not willing to talk about it—yet. She will, though. Make the effort to talk with her, about everything. I believe she will eventually share with you what's going on in her heart."

Garrett tipped his head, though he knew Lauren didn't know the whole truth. He knew Macy blamed him for Susie's death. She had every right to feel the way she did. It was his fault.

Lauren got up, brought the teapot over to the table and filled their cups.

"Thanks."

"I'm sorry you've got this whole contest thing going on while you're trying to straighten things out with Macy. Not exactly a good time to have strangers around." Lauren stirred some sugar into her tea and added a bit of milk.

He looked at her. "Actually, I'm really glad you're here, Lauren," he said, meaning every word. "You see things from a woman's perspective that I can't see." With a spoon he stirred milk into his own tea and took a drink. "I needed this. It's been a long day."

They talked a while longer, then Lauren said she had better get to bed. Funny how much more relaxed he felt now after talking with her. There was just something nice about sitting in the kitchen with her late at night over a cup of tea.

"Garrett, please don't get mad at me, but would you allow me to pray for you and Macy?"

He swallowed hard. She meant well. He knew she did. Still, pray to the God who had failed him?

"Of course, if you would rather I not…"

Yet something at the very core of him yearned for that kind of relationship with God once again. He had been a strong believer before… "Thanks, Lauren," he heard himself say. "He'll listen to you."

She placed her hand on his once again. Over the next few minutes she lifted her heart in prayer, asking God to bless their family, and asking Him to give Garrett wisdom in the situation with Macy. By the time she had finished praying, Garrett almost wished things could be as they were before. The way she talked to God made him remember when times were different. Yet his heart had grown so cold and hard, Garrett figured even God couldn't reach him now.

Chapter Eleven

The next morning Lauren woke up feeling light-hearted. The moments she had shared last night with Garrett over tea had warmed her heart in a real way. He had not only accepted her prayer but actually seemed to truly appreciate it. Lauren knew God was working in Garrett's and Macy's hearts, and Lauren's feelings for this family were definitely growing.

Sitting up in bed, she raised her arms in a full stretch, letting out a hearty yawn. Nocchi stirred in the bed on the floor beside Lauren and finally lifted her head. Lauren scooted off the mattress and scrunched down beside her dog.

"Good morning, girl," she said. Nocchi let out a yawn. Her tail wagged with as little energy as Lauren felt before her morning caffeine consumption. Lauren laughed. "Guess we both need our coffee this morning." She glanced at the clock. "Oh, dear, I'd better hurry or they'll go hiking without me."

Without another moment's hesitation Lauren scurried around the room, gathering her hiking clothes and the necessary items Garrett had mentioned the night before. If Candace and Gwen could see her today, they would never believe it. Lauren Romey actually going hiking in full mountain gear? Her chin rose a notch. Well, it was not as though she wasn't the adventurous type. So what if she happened to prefer working up a sweat in a sauna as opposed to hiking in the woods—was that so wrong? Laying out her clothes carefully on the bed, Lauren grabbed her essentials and headed for the bathroom.

Maybe she was a bit, well, citified. But at least she didn't whine about the idea the way Gracie did. Now, that wasn't to say Candace and Gwen wouldn't pay for putting her through this. She smiled in spite of herself. Oddly enough, she was actually looking forward to this little trek. After all, it's not like she was in bad shape. She made regular trips to the gym. But hiking on a mountain, with bears? That is *so* not her thing.

Lauren turned on the water in the shower. "Oh, well, this could be the beginning of a new adventure for me." As she stepped into the warmth of the steamy water, her voice lifted a song of praise in melody. She sang heartily, each note soaring with her spirit. She felt confident that neither the hiking trip nor the hot sun—in fact, not even Gracie Jane Skinner—could steal her joy today. The Lord had created this day and she was bound and determined to enjoy it. Come what may.

Once her shower was over, she quickly dressed and prepared to take Nocchi out. Lauren grabbed a casual T-shirt and shrugged it over Nocchi's head. Nocchi was ready to go. With a slight hesitation, Lauren dared a glance into the full-length mirror.

G.I. Joe with hair stared back at her.

She sighed, grabbed Nocchi's leash and stepped over to the door. Noticing a folded piece of paper on the floor, she bent and picked it up, noting her name on the front. She unfolded the paper.

"Lauren, would you do me the honor of having dinner with me tonight at seven o'clock? My plans are to take you to one of the finer restaurants in the Lake Tahoe area, if you don't mind. We can talk about it on the hiking trip. Can't wait. Garrett."

Her heart skipped as she reread the words *Can't wait.* She read it again. Another skip and a shiver.

Hold on. *Can't wait* as in looking forward to getting together? *Can't wait* as in I want to hurry up and get this over with? She chewed on her pinkie fingernail. Her thoughts clouded for a fraction of a heartbeat until she remembered her resolve to have a good day. She perked up again.

Oh, dear, she was beginning to act like Gwen.

She practically skipped over to her bed and carefully laid the paper down. She smoothed it out a couple of times. "Yep, this is going to be a good day," Lauren said with a grin she couldn't hide as she and Nocchi made their way out the door and down the stairs.

Once Nocchi had taken care of business and settled back in the room, Lauren went into the kitchen for a quick cup of coffee before their hiking trip. One glance at the others told her they weren't much for early-morning hours, either—all except Billie, but she didn't count. She was probably used to getting up at the crack of dawn and waiting in a tree stand for an elk to pass.

"Morning, Lauren." Billie was positively breathless with excitement.

"Well, howdy, Lucy," Gracie sneered. "I hope you can live without your coffee, because I just drank the last cup." She took another sip and licked her lips as if it was just the best little ol' cup of coffee she'd had in quite a spell.

Lauren's early-morning enthusiasm waned slightly. "Last cup?" She tried to say it as though it wouldn't bother her in the least, though the idea of hurting someone had crossed her mind.

"I'm sorry, Lauren. I meant to get some more last night, and I forgot," Macy said.

"Oh, that's fine, Macy." Lauren forced herself to be polite. It wasn't fine. No coffee? Did they know what they were asking here? How could she survive the morning—let alone the day—without coffee? Hot chocolate and tea wouldn't cut it. She needed coffee. Now. How could she climb the rugged mountain peaks, trek through rough terrain—leap tall buildings at a single bound? It was inhuman, that's what it was. Her good mood had definitely taken a nosedive. Someone had to pay.

"Hey, I know how you look forward to your morning cup of coffee. How about I run you over to the coffee shop?" Garrett offered.

"Thanks, but that's not necessary, Garrett. But if there is time, I might drive over myself," Lauren said.

He held up his hands. "I admit it. I had an ulterior motive. I want some myself." Garrett wiggled his eyebrows.

Lauren laughed—until she heard someone harrumph. She didn't have to turn around to see who it was. Only Gracie could harrumph that way. For some reason that sound made Lauren feel better. She knew she should be ashamed—but for now she soaked in it like a bubble bath.

"Okay."

"Great. Let's go. Molly, Macy, we'll be right back," Garrett called over his shoulder as he guided Lauren through the back door with his hand nudging her back midway.

Her good mood was back in place and she was feeling mighty fine.

Once they were in the car, Garrett brushed his hands together, started the engine and looked at her with a grin that made Lauren's heart leap to her throat.

"I can hardly wait for our hiking trip," he said.

Her heart dropped back into place. Somehow she managed to curve her mouth upward, and then turned to stare out her window. His sparkling eyes and energetic enthusiasm did not come from being with her. His excitement came from the idea of hiking—tromping over dirt. What did people see in that anyway? Exercise, blisters, tired muscles. Oh, yeah, loads of fun.

"You okay?"

Oh, sure, I'm fine. Give me a couple of hours of pain and sweat, and I'm deliriously happy.

"Lauren?"

His voice shook her free from her thoughts. She turned to him and pasted on a smile. "Uh, yes, I'm fine."

"Great."

Clueless. Completely clueless.

"I want to tell you how much I enjoyed our little tea escapade last night."

Her heart zipped back to her throat. A good sign. A very good sign.

"Me, too," she squeaked. What was she thinking? She had better back off. Too many differences between them. She'd been down this road before and had no intention of traveling it now. This was dangerous territory, definitely out of bounds. Not to mention that she hadn't given herself the promised year to heal.

Wait. Two friends—that's what they were fast becoming. Friends. Nothing wrong with that, right? People were supposed to reach out to others, love their neighbors as themselves and all that. She owed him that much.

"I'd forgotten how much I enjoyed quiet talks. I've been so caught up in my own world."

"It's understandable, Garrett."

"Maybe." Pulling into the parking spot at the coffee shop, he clicked off the ignition key and turned to her. He placed his hand on top of hers. "I want you to know how much I enjoyed it." Glistening brown eyes stared into hers.

What was that sound? Had she just gulped? Out loud? She was pretty sure she had heard someone gulp. And it seemed to have come from somewhere near the vicinity of her throat.

Friends, Lauren. Merely friends.

"Did you get my note about tonight?"

"Yes." Whew. He hadn't seemed to notice the gulp.

"We'll see how you feel after hiking. If you're too tired, we can go out tomorrow night. It's up to you."

"All right. Thanks."

Garrett squeezed her hand lightly. "Let's go get that coffee."

In no time they had their coffee and had arrived back at the house. Lauren smothered her amusement behind her hand when she saw the ladies in their hiking gear. A family of G.I. Joes. But Billie was a G.I. Joe all too happy to enlist. The others most definitely had been drafted.

After a quick breakfast Garrett gave last-minute instructions to Macy and Molly on the time and place for them to wait for the group after the hike.

He turned to the contestants. "Well, ladies, this is it," he said with a sort of sadistic drill-sergeant flair.

There was more to this man than met the eye.

A solemn lot, the ladies boarded the van. Lauren imagined a lone soldier playing taps in the background.

She *could* do this, right?

The fact that everyone kept quiet as the van headed north amused Garrett. Gracie had made it abundantly clear she did not look forward to the hiking trip. Lauren had been a bit more discreet, though he could see the disdain on her face. Citified, both of them. Not that he was trying to prove anything. He just thought it would be fun to hike together as a group and see how the ladies interacted with one another and with him.

He mentally shook his head. He had to stop thinking that way. It wasn't as though he wanted to pick someone special out of the group for himself. Goodness, he was beginning to think like Macy and Molly. His hands gripped the steering wheel. The sooner he got through this contest, the better. Peace and quiet would soon be his once again. The very idea made him feel better—until a vision of Lauren snuggling next to him by the fireplace on a wintry night hit him as hard as a two-by-four.

Whoa, what had prompted that? He thought back to their chat last night over tea. Something about her face, her laugh, the things she said, all stirred him in a way he hadn't felt in years. He sat up straight in his seat and rubbed the back of his neck. That kind of thinking had to stop. Now.

"You okay?" Lauren asked from the front passenger's seat.

"Yeah." He couldn't look at her.

Garrett drove the rest of the way while the others remained fairly quiet. He suspected they were asleep. Gracie answered his suspicion with a snore that sounded as though it had wrapped around the uvula in the back of her throat and hung on for dear life.

They stopped at a light and he locked eyes with Lauren. She muffled a laugh. He grinned. "We'd better let her sleep. We'll all be happier in the long run. Plus, she'll need all the strength she can get."

Lauren looked as though she wanted to laugh again, then thought better of it. He figured she was worried about the needing-strength part.

Something told him this could be the best of days or the worst of days.

Soon Garrett pulled the van into a parking lot near the beginning of the trail. Everyone climbed out and loaded up with their essentials for hiking—water bottles, extra socks, bandages, rain gear. Garrett slung a backpack across his broad shoulders. Lauren wondered how he could carry all that, but by the looks of his build, she assumed he hiked on a regular basis. While she certainly wasn't unfit, her gym workouts were more for stress than body management. Judging by her current stress level, she figured the hike might do her some good.

Once everyone had what they needed, Garrett closed and locked the van doors, then looked at the others. "You all ready?"

"Ready." Billie appeared as if this day couldn't get any better.

Nikki looked unhappy, but resigned. Gracie groaned. Ellen held on to her glasses while she kept her gaze to the ground like a bird in search of earthworms.

Garrett shifted the backpack on his shoulders. "Let's go."

The trail started at the edge of an alpine forest. The trees mercifully shielded them from the warmth of the sun. A slight chill rustled through the branches and the group stopped so everyone could pull on a sweater.

"This is exactly why you can't pay attention to the weatherman when you go hiking. You need to be prepared," Garrett said with all the authority of a scoutmaster.

Lauren longed to soak in a hot tub.

The women trudged along quietly at first as Garrett pointed out the plant life scattered about the forest. They were hard-pressed to keep in step with their leader, but he waited for no one, and since they obviously didn't want to get left behind, they pushed themselves.

As they continued, climbing and descending small

ridges, stopping to view the valleys, alpine meadows and glaciated mountain terrain, each one shed her sweater and dipped several times into her water supply. At the summit the trail opened into granite outcrops, then descended to a plateau overlooking a sparkling lake. The water looked cool and refreshing and Lauren wanted more than anything to jump in.

"It does look inviting, doesn't it?" Garrett asked, coming up behind her as everyone talked about the beautiful view. She wasn't sure if her goose bumps came from the view or his nearness.

She turned to him, mere inches from his face. Without looking, she took a step back, and would have plunged to a small drop-off had Garrett not caught her by the arm. "You all right?" he asked, pulling her up next to him, closer than before.

"Yes, th-thank you," she stammered. At least she didn't gulp this time. He held her captive as his eyes stared into hers. Neither breathed. Neither said a word.

A twig snapped behind them. "I said isn't the view just beautiful?" Gracie repeated with impatience.

Garrett kept his gaze fixed on Lauren. "Beautiful."

Gracie's gasp pulled them loose from whatever it was that had just happened between them. Garrett cleared his throat and walked away. Gracie stared daggers at Lauren, then followed him.

One thing Lauren knew—she did not want to be alone near a cliff while Gracie stood nearby.

After the group had trekked another mile or so, they came upon a breathtaking clearing with a lake more beautiful than the last. Settling on a grassy knoll just by the water's edge, they pulled out their lunches and rested there. Nikki fell into a heap with her backpack. Ellen sat down, barely making a ripple in the grass. Billie looked energized from their morning excursion, Gracie looked as though she might keel over from the sheer distress of it all and Lauren happily settled onto a small boulder.

Garrett watched them closely. Maybe he had worked them too hard. They obviously were not used to it. Well, except for Billie. That woman had the strength of a moose.

Everyone appeared too tired to talk as they pulled open their lunch bags and retrieved the lunches his girls had made. He couldn't have done all this without Macy and Molly. Of course, if not for Macy and Molly, he wouldn't be in this mess in the first place.

Garrett glanced over at Lauren and caught her praying for her meal. She didn't mind at all what the others thought. She was genuine. That's what he really appreciated about her.

He had been that way once upon a time. Genuine and sure in what he believed. Then everything had changed. It wasn't as if he didn't want to believe. He wanted to, but he couldn't. Besides, no one with any brains wants to get hurt. When you make yourself vulnerable by trusting and believing in someone, you're bound to get hurt. So he'd chosen to play it safe. Kept everyone, including God, at arm's length.

He glanced at Lauren again. She was threatening his safety. As much as he felt drawn to her, he had better guard himself. Nothing good could come of it.

Garrett knew that from experience.

After everyone finished their lunches, they pulled off

their socks and boots and dipped their feet in the water. They splashed the cool liquid on their faces and arms.

Soon they hiked the rest of the way to meet Macy at their rendezvous point. Everyone climbed into the van.

"Did Molly drive the other car home?" Garrett asked Macy as he settled into the passenger's seat.

"Yeah. She didn't want to drive the van, since she hasn't driven it all that much," Macy said.

"Thanks for coming to pick us up, Macy," Lauren said.

"No problem." Macy backed the van out of the parking space. "Did you have a good time?"

All the ladies indicated they had enjoyed the day, but Garrett suspected they would rather have had a root canal. Except for Billie.

Garrett looked back at Lauren. Her eyelids were drooping until she saw him looking at her, then she forced herself to attention.

He covered his amusement and rubbed his hand along his chin. "You know, I was thinking tomorrow night might be better for going out to dinner. What do you think?" he asked.

Lauren's shoulders visibly relaxed. "I think that would be great. I am pretty tired."

"Tomorrow it is." Feeling disappointed but being careful not to show it, he turned back around. Hadn't he decided he needed to be on guard? Here he was all too eager to set himself up for a fall once again. He clenched his jaw. Tomorrow night they would enjoy a friendly discussion over dinner.

Nothing more.

Chapter Twelve

Adding just the right touch to her navy pantsuit by putting on gold jewelry, Lauren stood back and looked in the mirror. Feeling satisfied with her appearance, she grabbed her handbag. Someone knocked at her door.

She glanced around the room to make sure she had what she needed, then answered. Macy and Molly stood smiling in the doorway.

"Wow, you look great," Molly said, eyes wide.

Macy agreed. "We knew Dad was taking you out tonight, and well, we just wanted to wish you a good time."

"We can tell he cares a lot about you," Molly said, wiggling her eyebrows.

Macy nudged Molly.

"Well, I appreciate the thought, girls. I'm sure we'll have a fine time." Lauren winked and gave them both a quick hug.

Macy took a step back. "We just wanted you to know, that, um, we hope you have a good time."

"Thanks." Lauren watched as they turned and walked down the hallway. She was touched by their gesture. For reasons unknown to her, she had bonded with Macy and Molly. She felt a genuine compassion for these girls and prayed God's best for them.

She walked down the stairs and into the great room, where the other ladies had gathered. Gracie flipped through a fashion magazine. Nikki looked up from a vegetarian cookbook. "Oh, you going out?"

"Yeah. Guess it's my turn." Lauren felt kind of silly saying that. It seemed strange to go out with a man she knew everyone else was dating, too.

"Have a great time," Nikki said.

"Well, honey, you'd better hope he doesn't get a headache and cut it short, the way he did with me," Gracie said with a bitter edge.

"Who wouldn't get a headache with you," Nikki mumbled.

"What did you say?" Gracie demanded.

"Sometimes you get a headache from food."

Billie and Nikki snickered. Ellen kept her nose in a book.

"You ready?" Garrett's voice called behind her.

Lauren turned to face him. The look on his face made her glad she had purchased the pantsuit. He looked every bit as delighted to see her as he had the first time he caught her in it.

"You look incredible," he said for her ears alone.

Her face burned with the compliment. "Thanks."

"Good night all," he called over his shoulder as they headed toward the door.

Lauren couldn't help but feel a little giddy with the prospect of their date.

Friends. Merely friends, she reminded herself. But she couldn't deny the feeling of wishing it could be more.

"Did you bring along a jacket, the way I asked you?" Garrett asked.

"Yep." Lauren lifted the jacket in her right arm. She looked at him with a mischievous grin. "You're not going to tell me what this is about, are you?"

Garrett shook his head. "Nope. You have to wait till we get there."

Lauren settled into her seat. Garrett glanced at her, thinking she looked happy, eager even, for their evening together. What woman didn't enjoy surprises?

Garrett, ol' boy, you're doing all right. He shifted back in his seat, feeling mighty fine. He thought a moment. Maybe it wasn't fair to the others. He had planned only dinners out with them, but he had to admit Lauren had become a special friend in the short time he had known her. His girls got along with her, and whenever his teenagers got along with anyone, he figured it was a real plus. They had been hesitant about other women in the past. And there had been several who had pursued him after his wife's death. Macy and Molly had resented that, but they didn't need to worry. He hadn't been interested. He didn't want to be interested now, but Lauren had captured his attention. After all, this wasn't a life commitment; it was a two-week friendship. It wouldn't last beyond that. They had too many miles between them. This was a safe relationship that he could pursue for now. Have fun without all the entanglements of a romantic relationship.

"Have you been able to rest at all since you've been here?" Garrett asked.

"I've had a nice time. I really have," Lauren said. "The days are going faster than I had expected."

"That's a good sign, isn't it?" Garrett asked with grin.

"Depends on how you look at it."

"Oh?"

"Well, I guess it means I'm having a good time, but it also means I'll soon have to get back and look for a job."

"Is that all?"

"What do you mean?" she asked.

"Is that all it means?" Garrett pressed.

"Yes—no—I don't understand," she stammered.

They stopped for a traffic light and he turned to her. "Are you sad at all?"

"Sad?"

"That you'll be leaving in a week? It will all be over?"

"Should I be?"

"Well, I kind of hoped you would be. I know I will be—when it's all over, I mean," he said, surprising himself. He felt a little adventurous tonight, as if he could really express himself with little fear since they only had a week longer together. No commitments, just purely enjoying the now.

He could feel her staring at him and he basked in it. He wanted to fill her night with puzzles and surprises. They traveled a while longer, passing mountainous vistas shrouded in twilight, discussing the landscape and life in the Lake Tahoe area in general.

Finally they pulled up to the parking lot at Ski Run Marina Village in South Lake Tahoe. Lauren looked around. Garrett pointed to the *Tahoe Queen,* an authentic Mississippi paddle wheeler.

Lauren turned to him. "We're taking the *Tahoe Queen?*" Her eyes were expressive, sparkling.

"Their dinner boat cruise. Do you mind?" He held his breath as he awaited her response.

"Mind? I love it!"

He released his breath and relaxed. *Garrett, you're the man, dude. You've done well,* he told himself. He gave himself a mental pat on the back, then said, "Great! Let's go."

They got out of the car and headed toward the *Queen.* "I haven't done this in a long time," he said.

"Garrett, this is perfect. The lake is beautiful in the daytime, and I imagine just as beautiful at night." Her lips curved upward as she looked at him. "Thank you."

A weird feeling shot through him, surging through his veins like a wild roller coaster. He felt invigorated, carefree, wonderful.

They handed the man their ticket and stepped up the ramp to the boat. Lauren turned to Garrett. "After dinner can we sit out on the top level?" Her eyes were so vibrant, expressive—pools of excitement into which he wanted to step.

Garrett grinned. "If that's what you want. You sure you won't be too cold?"

Lauren held up her jacket. "I'll just put this on."

Garrett was very glad he had decided on this for their evening together.

Yes, their evening held promise.

* * *

Lauren held up her hand. "Oh my, after that four-course meal, I couldn't eat another bite."

"I'm pretty stuffed myself," Garrett said, patting his stomach.

The water lapped against the boat, rocking it in a comforting rhythm. Lauren couldn't remember the last time she had enjoyed such an evening with a man. Her thoughts ran to Jeff, but she quickly dismissed them. Funny how his face now faded from remembrance. She had thought she would never be able to erase his blue eyes—were they blue?—from her memory.

"You enjoying yourself?" Garrett asked.

"Mmm, very much," she said, looking from the window to him.

"Want to go up on the top deck now?"

"That would be great." Garrett helped her drape her jacket around her shoulders and they climbed the steps to the top level. Shadowy views of beautiful scenery played off the lights from the boat. A full moon glistened overhead, its reflection trailing behind the paddle wheel like the train of a wedding gown.

Garrett and Lauren sat on a bench near the side railing. The brisk night air brushed against Lauren's face, causing her skin to tingle. There was only a smattering of couples on the top deck, all appearing lost in each other. Most had chosen to stay below and listen to a mariachi band perform. Lauren took a deep breath of the misty air that mingled with the musky scent she had come to associate with Garrett. For the first time in months she was actually able to truly relax and enjoy herself.

A cool breeze stirred past them, causing Lauren to shiver. She stretched out her arm to pull on her jacket.

"Here, let me help you with that." Garrett held her jacket in place while she tucked her arms into the sleeves. She settled back into her seat and he reached behind her, gently lifting her hair from the collar of the jacket. His fingers brushed against the back of her neck, causing another shiver.

She looked at him. "Thank you," she said, tilting her face up to him.

Their eyes locked. His hand lay softly against her neck, without the slightest movement. Lauren forced herself to breathe. With his right hand Garrett reached up and stroked the side of her face as he leaned toward her, closer with every heartbeat. His hand on her neck pushed her toward him ever so gently. His eyes told her he'd longed for this moment and the time was right. Wrapped in shadows beneath the moonlight and twinkling stars, Garrett's mouth pressed tenderly upon hers with only a hint of the deep emotion he seemed to be holding at bay. His hand worked its way through the back of her hair as she surrendered to his embrace, the warmth of his touch, the softness of his lips, breathless with the wonder of it all. When he finally broke away, he stroked the side of her face once more, his gaze all the while holding hers. Though he said nothing, his dark, compelling eyes told her everything she longed to hear.

The water sloshed against the boat while they lost themselves in the moment. Garrett settled back against the bench. His arm still around Lauren, he pulled her to him and she snuggled next to his chest, thankful for the warmth and his nearness. As she kept her eyes on the mountain peaks silhouetted against the night sky, her heart whispered warnings, but she shut them out. She wanted to linger in the moment, not let anything ruin it. Didn't she deserve that much after all she had been through?

Garrett stared across the waters, but saw nothing. His heart was telling him something he refused to believe. He hadn't kissed a woman in three years—of course his emotions would go crazy. It was nothing more than that. Right?

Not that he didn't care for Lauren. He did, much more than he wanted to admit. But he had no desire to get into another relationship only to lose someone he loved—again. What was he worried about? Lauren would be leaving in a week, and he would never see her again. End of story. For some reason, that thought didn't make him feel any better.

"The mountains are so beautiful," Lauren said barely above a whisper as she leaned farther into him.

He tightened his arm around her, feeling strong and manly next to her small, delicate frame.

"I can't look at them without thinking of how majestic God is," Lauren said as if lost in thought. Then she looked up at him with a start. "Oh, I'm sorry, Garrett. I'm not trying to offend you. It's just that, well, He is just such a part of who I am."

"I know, Lauren." He squeezed her arm and glanced upward. "I used to feel that way once." He hadn't meant to say that out loud, and wished he could take it back. He didn't feel comfortable making himself vulnerable to anyone.

"I know some things are hard to understand, and I don't have all the answers. But we're caught up in this world together. Bad things happen to good people. What one person does affects another."

His gut tightened. He didn't want to talk about this. Not now. Not ever. "What good is a God who isn't there for you when you need Him?"

"Is that the reason you gave your life to Him, so He would do everything for you, your way?"

Though her voice was gentle, the truth of her words slammed into his chest.

"Aren't we to give our lives to Him to love and serve Him unconditionally, come what may?" she asked, her eyes searching into his soul for answers.

"Lauren, I can't talk about it."

"But that's the only way you will find your way back, Garrett."

He knew she meant well, but she was venturing into a place where he allowed no one to go. He didn't need her or anyone else telling him how he should live. He took his arm from her shoulders and looked at his watch. The evening would be over soon.

One week and he wouldn't have to think about this anymore. Lauren Romey would be gone, and he could go back to his routine.

Living in a cocoon, ignoring the truth?

What made him think that? Lauren was making him crazy. Trying to push him to believe things her way. Well, he was doing fine on his own.

"I'm sorry, Garrett" was all Lauren said when she saw him glance at his watch. Though he was sure the look on her face would haunt him for days to come.

The rest of the evening passed in a blur, and he couldn't get home fast enough.

To the safety of his cocoon.

Lauren kept her tears in check the rest of her evening with Garrett. Everything had been perfect until she'd made that comment about God. When would she learn to stop blabbing on and on? She didn't have to save the world. She didn't even have to save Garrett. Nor could she.

After her nightly bedtime ritual, she climbed into bed beneath the covers.

The night had been so perfect up to that point. She had discovered one thing, though. She now knew she was in love.

With Garrett Cantrell.

How was that possible? They had known each other only a week. But of course, their week together had been constant, so it seemed as though they had known each other for a much longer period of time. Still, she had promised herself she would wait a year before allowing her heart to take a leap into a new relationship.

Now what?

She adjusted to a comfortable position. She could not allow herself to get involved with Garrett knowing how he felt about God. That was an absolute. Wait. She was already involved. So where would they go from here?

Nowhere.

Her heart sank. She tried to persuade God to make it all work, but hours later when she finally drifted off to sleep, the answer was all too clear.

God came first. She would have to give up Garrett Cantrel.

Chapter Thirteen

Garrett punched his pillow into place for the umpteenth time and tried to get comfortable. Who was he kidding? He couldn't sleep. He yanked off the covers and sat at the edge of his bed.

Everything had gone well tonight until Lauren had to bring God into the mix. Before she came along Garrett had been content in his decision to leave God out of his life. He would not make a decision of faith based on his feelings for a woman, that was for sure.

He had to admit what she had said made sense, though he refused to dwell on it. The thought of calling his pastor came to him. They had been close friends before Susie's death, but Garrett had closed Pastor Burke out of his life, too. He raked his fingers through his hair and sighed. He had made such a mess of things.

Garrett got down on the floor and reached under the bed for the box holding his Bible. He pulled open the lid and looked at the leather-bound cover. Was this the very book that he had lifted from his bedside stand each night, drawing strength from its pages? He curled his fingers around the binding and lifted it from the box. Funny how after all this time it still felt warm and familiar. In the quiet, he leafed through the pages, glancing at the underlined Scriptures and notes he had written in the margins.

Susie's sweet face popped into his mind, causing an instant chill to his heart. He dropped the Bible back into the box, returned the lid to its place and shoved everything under the bed. He wasn't ready to rethink his decision. Not yet.

He wasn't sure he would ever be ready.

The next morning Garrett hurried to get dressed and have breakfast on the table for the ladies so everyone could make it to church on time. He was glad he didn't always have to worry about that many women getting ready to go somewhere simultaneously. No doubt about it, having a houseful of women was taking its toll on him.

His daughters would pay—but then there was that bass boat he was still hoping he'd get for his great attitude about the contest.

A white clapboard church, complete with steeple and bell, stood before them as Garrett, his daughters and the contestants stepped out of the car. They made their way inside, shuffled across the wooden floor, and finally settled into an empty wooden pew. It was a no-frills kind of place, which suited Garrett just fine.

The organ music started, and though Lauren sat beside Macy who sat beside him, Garrett could still hear her beautiful soprano voice rising in worship. He dared a glance her way and could tell she meant every word she sang.

He tried to ignore the way the sunlight played upon her hair, the way her turquoise top accentuated the color of her eyes. He didn't want to think of that now. He had no right. Especially here. In the very church where he and Susie had married long ago.

Their morning conversation with Lauren had been tense at best. Just no way to break down the wall between them. Not that it mattered. If he did care for her in *that* way, she could never be happy tucked away in an alpine forest at a bed-and-breakfast. And of course there was that whole religion thing. No way to fix that. If he did care for her that way.

Which he didn't.

Pastor Paul Burke read from the Scriptures and talked about God's ways not being man's ways. Garrett felt the sermon directed toward him and wondered if Lauren had talked to the pastor. He half expected her to look at him, but she didn't, not even once.

After the service was over, Garrett sought out and found Pastor Burke. The pastor had just finished shaking someone's hand, then turned to see Garrett.

"How have you been?" he asked, grabbing Garrett's hand and giving it a hearty shake.

"Doing pretty good."

"Hey, I've missed our lunches, guy," he said with a teasing grin.

"Um, that's why I wanted to talk to you. Wondered if we could have lunch one day next week?"

The pastor didn't skip a beat. "You got it. How about tomorrow?"

His response surprised Garrett. He had thought Paul would put him off for a couple of weeks. Hadn't he put the pastor off for the past three years?

"That would be great." They discussed when and where they would meet.

The pastor leaned into Garrett. "By the way, that's a fine group of ladies you have with you this morning," he said with a wink. Paul was a bachelor, never married.

Garrett hadn't thought of how it must look—him attending church with five ladies. He opened his mouth, but the pastor raised a hand.

"No need to explain." He laughed. "I saw it on the news. Great coverage, by the way."

Garrett grimaced. Drew Huntington. News reporter, aka dead meat if he didn't stay away from Macy.

"Pretty smart girls you've got there, that Macy and Molly." He winked again.

"Want to adopt them?"

At this, the pastor let out an energetic laugh. "Sorry. My dog keeps me busy enough as it is."

Now, there was an idea. Next time Macy and Molly felt adventurous, he'd ask them to just give him another dog.

Lauren peeked out her window in time to see Garrett leaving with Nikki for their evening together. Lauren wondered if he would treat Nikki to a dinner cruise on the *Tahoe Queen,* too. She tried not to think about it. Nikki looked very nice in her green top and black pants.

And Garrett—well, George Clooney had nothing on him. Speaking of which, Lauren still wanted to see one of George's movies. First thing when she got home, she'd pull a DVD from her collection, sit down with a bowl of popcorn and indulge.

Lauren stepped away from the window, changed into some comfortable sweats and headed downstairs. Popcorn sounded good. When she walked into the great room, Ellen was sitting in a chair, reading a book. Just beyond her, a low crackling fire from the hearth absorbed the night's chill and filled the air with the smell of pine.

"Hey, Lauren," Billie called out, glancing away for a moment from the suspense movie on TV.

"Want some popcorn? I thought I would make some."

"No, thanks. I've had enough to eat today," said Billie, ever the fitness queen.

Lauren turned away. Truth was she had eaten too much today as well, but she felt rebellious tonight. If she spotted any chocolate in the house, she was prepared to offer big bucks for it.

Chocolate was her comfort food in hard times. In her book, it was a staple that she couldn't live without. When she had found Jeff and Camilla together, she'd gone home and almost eaten herself into a chocolate coma. She felt its medicinal potential was way underrated.

Ambling into the kitchen, she pulled out the popcorn from the bin where Garrett had showed them to help themselves. Opening the outer package, she pulled off the cellophane, plunked the bag into the microwave, set the timer and grabbed a glass from the cabinet. Filling her glass with ice, she plucked a soft drink from the fridge and listened to it fizz and snap as it wandered over the ice.

"Hi, Lauren."

She turned to see Macy and Molly behind her, smiling.

"Hi, girls. What are you up to?"

"We're bored," Molly said with a frown.

Macy made a face to emphasize the point.

"Hmm, that is a problem." Lauren thought a moment. "Want some popcorn?"

"Hey, that sounds good," Molly said, retrieving a bowl from the cabinet.

Macy followed suit.

"Tell you what—I was getting ready to take some up to my room. Want to join me? We can have a gab fest."

"Really?" Macy asked, excitement sparkling in her eyes.

"Really."

"Is it okay if I get comfortable and put on my pajamas first?" Molly asked.

"This early?" Macy looked at her sister in surprise.

"Why not? We're not going anywhere. We can have a girls' slumber party where we sit around and eat and talk and talk and eat."

No doubt about it—that was Lauren's kind of party. She wondered if she should ask about chocolate, then thought better of it.

"Okay, I think I will, too, then. Be right back," Macy said as they both headed out the door.

Lauren grinned as she watched them. She cared about those girls—she cared about them a lot. The timer went off on the microwave. Dumping the popcorn into a big bowl, she scooped up some napkins, picked up her drink and headed for her room. She actually looked forward to this little girl-talk session.

Besides, it would keep her mind off Garrett and Nikki.

The server placed Nikki's and Garrett's ordered meals in front of them and walked away. After flipping the cloth napkin onto his lap, Garrett cut into his steak. This place was known for its top-of-the-line beef, and he could hardly wait to sink his teeth into it. Spearing a piece of meat with his fork, he had opened his mouth and was preparing to take a bite when he got a look at Nikki. The expression on her face said she had seen a ghost. The chunk of beef hovered near his lips.

"You're going to eat that?" She pointed to the meat.

"Well, that was the plan." He lowered his fork and hesitated. "Is something wrong?"

Her mouth puckered, and her chin quivered.

"What is it?"

"Do you know that beef was somebody's baby? One minute he was happily grazing in a grassy field with his family and friends, and the next he was whisked off to a slaughterhouse where unspeakable horrors took place right in front of his eyes."

Openmouthed, Garrett stared at her. He looked from Nikki to the meat, and back to Nikki. He swallowed hard and returned his fork to the plate, feeling a little less than hungry.

"I just don't understand how people can do that to animals."

It took him a minute to digest what had just

happened here. He wanted to change the subject and take the focus off his meal. "So tell me about yourself, Nikki," he said with as cheerful a voice as he could muster, all the while trying to rid his mind of the happy cow family grazing in the pasture.

She blinked, then picked up her fork, gathering some lettuce leaves on the end of the prongs. "Oh, not a lot to tell, really. I'm vegetarian, as you probably guessed if you didn't know it already."

Great. He forgot she was a vegetarian. The best steak house in town, and I had to bring the meat warden. He looked with longing at the steak on his plate, wondering if he could sneak a bite when she wasn't looking.

She didn't seem to notice his discomfort, and continued on. "Let's see, I collect and sell vintage clothes on the Internet. Um—" she waved her empty fork in the air "—I'm an environmentalist at heart." Stabbing some more lettuce, she looked up and leaned into the table. "Did you see the movie *Revenge of the Trees?*"

Too bad, he had missed that one. He shook his head.

"Oh, my goodness! You talk about scary!" She clicked her tongue, then took a bite of salad.

Without moving an inch, Garrett looked out of his peripheral vision on either side to make sure no one nearby was listening.

"I believe that could happen, though," she finally said.

He stared, gaped and swallowed.

"The total takeover of trees, I mean. We need to take care of Mother Earth," she said, stabbing the air with her fork. "You mark my words." She dished out some alfalfa sprouts.

Okay, he loved nature as much as the next person, but he just wasn't relating here.

Happily chewing on her salad, she looked around the room, seemingly oblivious to the fact Garrett was staring at her.

Garrett looked back at the tender steak on his plate. His favorite cut. He had looked forward to tonight and this melt-in-your-mouth meat. Now when he looked at it, he could see the happy Cattle family frolicking in the fields. Did he hear a bell clink? He looked around. No, no, just silverware. A cold sweat broke out on his forehead. He pushed aside his plate.

Nikki looked at him in all innocence. "Aren't you hungry?"

She was kidding, right? He watched as she munched on her salad and wondered if she realized she was robbing baby bunnies of their lettuce leaves.

He wasn't sure even the bass boat could make up for this. His girls were going to pay.

Lauren placed her soft drink on a coaster on the stand next to her bed and settled onto the mattress. A knock sounded at the door.

"Come in."

Macy and Molly came in chattering excitedly as they carried their bowls, drinks and pillows.

"Now, don't worry," Molly said, "We're not going to sleep in your room. We just wanted to get comfortable."

Lauren laughed. "Great." She patted a place on her comforter. "Come on over." She took their bowls and filled them with popcorn. "Good thinking," Lauren said when she saw Macy step outside the door and retrieve a small folding table.

They settled in, crossed their legs and started munching popcorn while Nocchi looked on, no doubt hoping they'd drop a morsel or two.

"So, tell me what you two have been up to today," Lauren said.

"I've been looking over college brochures." Molly crunched on some popcorn and rolled her eyes. "It's so hard to decide."

"Do you want to stay close to home, or do you have a preference?" Lauren asked.

"I'll probably just end up going to Armstrong University. It's about four hours away, so that wouldn't be too bad. I want to major in business management, plus I want to stay fairly close to home so I can check on Dad."

"Where are you going to college next year, Macy?"

"The same. Armstrong."

"Have you decided on a major?"

"Business." Macy said the word with little enthusiasm.

"Business is a good field. I majored in business before going on to law school. Sounds as though the bed-and-breakfast has affected your future," Lauren said, shoving some popcorn into her mouth.

"We want to help Dad as much as we can. We worry about him." Molly reached for her glass on the TV tray and took a drink.

"Does he know that?" Lauren asked. "I mean, are those the majors you really want, or do you feel you need those majors to help your dad with the business?"

Macy and Molly shared a glance, but said nothing.

"Okay, what gives?" Lauren prodded.

"I guess I'd rather teach. But Dad needs us. He can't run the business by himself," Macy said. "I mean, he lives on his investments, so he doesn't need the money, but he still wants to keep this place going—I think he does it for Mom. She had always wanted a bed-and-breakfast."

A moment of silence passed between them.

"Can't he hire help?" Lauren asked.

"Sure he can. That's what he'll have to do while we're away at school. But it just seemed we ought to keep it in the family," Molly said.

"Is this what you want to do, Molly?"

She nodded. "I've wanted to go into business management since I organized my first tea party as a kid." She laughed.

"Well, that's good." Lauren turned to Macy. "But do you think your dad would want you to go into a field of study for him and not pursue your own passion?"

Macy didn't say anything.

"Of course he wouldn't want her to do that," Molly said. "But she's stubborn. Feels she owes him something."

Macy shot a don't-go-there look at her sister.

Molly backed off and scooped a handful of popcorn into her mouth.

Curious. Lauren wondered what that was all about. She didn't want to overstep her bounds, but she wanted to help the girls in any way she could.

"You know, Macy, if you were my daughter, I would want you to pursue your dreams. From what I know of your dad, I think he would want the same."

Macy shook her head. "I have to do this."

"Why?"

"Because—because—" She looked at Molly, then glanced down at her popcorn bowl.

"She feels responsible for Mom's death," Molly blurted out.

Macy's head shot up. "Molly!"

"Well, you do. And you shouldn't. It wasn't your fault."

Lauren felt as though she had stumbled onto a family secret. She didn't want to pry, but she did want to help Macy work through her fears. "Macy, why would you feel that way?"

"No offense, Lauren, but I'd rather not talk about it."

"Okay." They continued to munch on popcorn, no one saying anything for a few minutes.

"So, tell me, how are things going with Drew Huntington?" Lauren teased, trying to take the tension from the room.

Macy brightened. "It's going well. We have a good time together."

"Wouldn't it be funny if Macy ended up marrying a news reporter?"

"Molly, don't say that! If Dad heard you, he would freak out!"

Molly grimaced. "Chill out. Dad isn't going to hear me."

"Well, still. I don't want you to slip and scare him. Besides, we're not dating that seriously."

"Yet," Molly said with stubborn insistence.

Macy gave her a look of warning.

"So how did your date go with Dad last night?"

"Molly! That's none of our business."

"No, it's okay," Lauren said. "We had a nice time."

"Really?" Excitement sparkled in Molly's eyes.

With a little hesitation, Lauren nodded.

"Uh-oh, there's something you're not telling us," Molly persisted.

"Well, let's just say we have some differences."

"Oh, the technology stuff." Molly took another drink.

"Technology stuff?" Lauren was confused.

"Dad says you and he are very different. You know, you prefer big-city stuff, and he wants the woods, country air, quiet nights at home, that sort of thing." Molly wiped her hands on a napkin.

Lauren sat speechless. He'd actually discussed her with the girls. She didn't know what to make of it. "Well, I don't know that we're all that different. I enjoy modern conveniences, that's true, but I enjoy quiet things, as well. It depends on where I am and who I'm with." She didn't miss the fact that the girls exchanged a glance.

"What was the problem then, last night—I mean, if you don't mind my asking?" Macy ventured.

"Well, it's complicated," Lauren said, tracing the stitching on the comforter with her finger. She looked up and found both girls watching her intently.

"You like him, don't you?" Molly asked, her eyebrows pulled into a worried expression.

Lauren nodded. "A lot."

Molly's shoulders relaxed.

"He's going to kill us when this contest is all over," Macy said.

Lauren grinned. "You think?"

"For sure."

"I'm sure he knows you were just trying to help."

"I don't think he sees it that way. What's up with that

Gracie chick, anyway?" Molly asked, putting her glass back on the stand and stretching her legs on the bed.

Lauren shrugged.

"Why, if I don't find myself a man—" Molly pressed the back of her hand to her forehead "—I just don't know what I'll do with my little ol' self."

Macy giggled. "Molly, that's not very nice."

Lauren ate some more popcorn to keep from laughing.

"Well, good grief, the woman needs a life. It's only too obvious she's trying to snag a man. Any man."

"I think Ellen is pretty, but she reminds me of a nervous Chihuahua," Macy said.

At this they all laughed.

"And Billie could wrestle Godzilla," Molly said.

"Don't forget Nikki. We'll pay for that one, all right. Dad and Goth Girl?" Macy shook her head.

"Never happen," Molly insisted.

Lauren rather enjoyed this conversation. She felt as though they were part of a family. With no sisters and brothers of her own, she enjoyed the feel of this.

"We messed up big-time," Macy said, shaking her head and leaning back on her elbows.

"It's the thought that counts," Lauren assured them.

"Well, at least he's enjoying you," Macy said.

The comment made Lauren's heart somersault. The surprise must have registered on her face.

"You knew that, right? I mean, it's only too obvious. You're the first woman Dad has shown an interest in since..." Molly let the words fall. "So you're cool with Dad?"

"Molly! You're prying again," Macy scolded.

"It's okay," Lauren said with a chuckle. "And the answer is yes." She couldn't tell them of the huge discrepancy in their faith. After all, Garrett tried to give a semblance of faith for the girls' sake. She didn't want them to know the truth. It could shake their own faith.

"I knew it!" Molly said with a clap.

"Well, we're not exactly hearing wedding bells, but we're friends," Lauren said, to calm down Molly's enthusiasm just a tad.

The trio talked a while longer, discussing boys, fashion and life at the B and B. Before they knew it, the car pulled up outside.

Molly scrambled from the bed and peeked out the window. "It's Dad and Nikki." She turned to Macy. "Want to go see how it went?"

"With Dad and Nikki? No way. I'm going to bed before he has a chance to pull us into the den and give us what for." Macy got up from the bed and gathered her bowl and glass.

"Tell you what—you girls go on to bed. I'll take care of the dishes."

"We don't want you to do that," Macy said.

Molly's expression told Macy to be quiet.

"It's no problem." Lauren ushered them through her door. "Thanks for the talk, girls. I really enjoyed it."

Macy turned to her and gave her a hug, then Molly walked over and did the same. Lauren's heart squeezed. She would miss these girls terribly when she went back home. After their embrace, the girls went to their rooms and Lauren glanced at the stairway in time to see Garrett standing there looking at her.

He had seen her with his girls, and the look on his face said he wasn't happy about it.

Chapter Fourteen

Garrett continued to stare long after Lauren had closed her door. He couldn't believe what he had just witnessed. His girls actually hugging her? They hardly knew her. Macy and Molly normally withheld such emotion until people earned their trust. He turned and trudged toward the den. Vegetarians, cross-eyed dogs, elk chasers.

Nothing made sense anymore.

After shuffling a few bills around on his desk, Garrett heard someone's footsteps in the hallway. He was still hungry, since Nikki had seen to it that he wasted a perfectly good piece of steak. Standing, he decided to go into the kitchen and see what he could find.

With the chance he might run into Lauren, he straightened his hair with a comb and retucked his shirt into his pants. A quick spray with a breath freshener and he was out the door. Hearing dishes clanking and the sound of tap water, he knew whoever it was had gone into the kitchen. He followed the sound, praying all the while that it wasn't Nikki or Gracie.

"Hi," he said with relief upon seeing Lauren at the sink.

"Hi, yourself." She was up to her elbows in soap bubbles.

"You're a guest here, remember?" he asked, deciding he'd get something to eat later. Instead, he opened a drawer and reached for a dry towel.

"I've never been good at sitting around and being waited on."

Well, he had to admit that surprised him. He thought big-city girls and pampering went hand in hand.

"I know what you're thinking."

He looked up with surprise.

"You're thinking that because I go to the spa and get my nails done professionally, I'm spoiled. Well, I'm not. Those are just luxuries I allow myself because I work hard." She rinsed out the popcorn bowl and laid it on the dry rack for him. "Okay, I probably shouldn't be indulging while I'm out of a job, but I know I'll get another one soon."

With appreciation, Garrett noted her confidence. He admired that in a woman. "I'm sure you will." He picked up the bowl and began to dry. "So have you had time to think about where you want to get a job next?"

"You mean townwise or companywise?"

Studying her for a second or two, he opened a cabinet and stacked the bowl in its appropriate place. "Either."

"I'm thinking about relocating."

He quirked an eyebrow.

"What, do you think that's a bad idea?"

"No, of course not. Now is the time to do it while you're single and have no ties."

She bit her lip.

Smooth going, Garrett. As if she needed to be reminded of her ex-fiancé. He looked at her closely. "I think it's a good idea. I really do." Picking up a smaller bowl, he dried it. "You know, Bliss Village could always use a good attorney." He grinned and winked at her. Good grief, what was he thinking? She prefers big cities, you dope. Get it through your head. Not that it mattered. Why would he want her here anyway? It wasn't as though they had a future together.

"So would you be my first client?" she teased.

"Sure, I would. Though I admit I hope I wouldn't need your services all that much."

"I'm a corporate attorney. I don't do criminal work, so you should be safe to work with me." She continued to tease.

"Well, okay, in that case, I will be happy to see you." He laughed. "You said your friends set you up to come here. Why Bliss Village?"

"Candace grew up here, and the three of us come here once a year to meet and catch up with one another's lives."

"That's pretty neat," he said, though he barely heard her. His mind had drifted to how things could be if she lived in Bliss Village.

"We love it here."

That brought his attention back around. Did she say she loved it here? "Really?"

She looked at him and laughed. "What? Are you surprised by that?"

"Frankly, yes. I mean, it doesn't offer the lures of the big-city lights and all."

She took the stopper from the sink and let the water drain. "Could I use your towel?"

Garrett handed it to her. Lauren lifted her hands from the dishwater and dried them. "Thanks." She returned the towel to him and sprayed the remaining bubbles from the sink for a clean rinse. "I know you have the idea I'm all about—" she gestured air quotes "—big city, but there's a lot more to me than you realize."

"I'm not saying it's a bad thing to enjoy the big city." He picked up the last pieces of silverware and dried them.

"And I do enjoy the conveniences of a large city, no question about it. But I also appreciate small-town living, to a degree. Still, let's face it, small towns don't offer young people a whole lot of, well, excitement."

Garrett frowned.

She stared at him. "Don't take offense. I'm not talking about Bliss Village. This is the exception. My goodness, who wouldn't love it here? Picturesque views at every turn, skiing, mountain climbing, you name it."

He didn't buy it. "Well, it's not exactly a thrill a moment for people who are used to shows, the hustle-bustle of shopping, the big corporate jobs."

"Nevada offers the nightlife, if a person wanted it. As for the big jobs, well, it's a give-and-take thing. It's different for each person—depends on what they really want. Besides, Tahoe isn't that far away."

"And what do you want, Lauren?"

She looked at him. "I don't know yet." Reaching for a glass, she poured herself some water and took a drink.

He looked at her, really looked at her, trying to figure

out how she really felt about Bliss Village. "So are you saying it's possible you could live in a place such as this?" He walked to the table and sat down in a chair, trying to act as though her answer wouldn't bother him either way.

She walked over and sat in front of him. "I haven't really thought about it. I mean, it's a long way from home." Her eyes took on a distant look.

A long way from her ex-fiancé is what she means, he thought. "Didn't you tell me your parents now live in Florida?"

"They do. And I probably will relocate, but such as it is, Indiana is still my home."

His spirits plunged. Just when he thought he was getting somewhere. Course, they still had their differences on how they felt about God. No doubt her thoughts had turned to her ex-fiancé. "Well, I'm sure you'll find the right place that suits you," he said, trying to act nonchalant. "So what was going on with you and my girls tonight?" he asked, wanting to get off their current subject.

She brightened. "Oh, we had a great time together."

He watched her expression, her hands moving with animation as she told him about her evening with the girls. He could tell Lauren, Macy and Molly were actually bonding, though he wasn't sure how he felt about that. After all, Lauren would be leaving by the end of the week. Then what? He grew pensive.

"They'll miss you, you know." He drew an invisible design on the table with his fingers.

"I know," she whispered. "I'll miss them, too."

"Is that all?" He looked at her.

Her head shot up. "What do you mean?"

"It's just that I was hoping you might..." He looked down at his fingers once again.

"Yes?"

"Oh, nothing." Silence stretched between them for the span of a heartbeat. He glanced at the clock in the kitchen. "Guess I should let you get to bed. I've kept you up long enough already." He stood to leave.

Lauren stood, looking perplexed.

Garrett felt awkward, not sure exactly how to cut things off. But he had to leave before he said something he would regret. Something that would give away his heart. A heart that told him something he hadn't wanted to face before now. He cared about Lauren Romey more than he wanted to admit. And he held out no hope for a relationship with her.

He turned to head out of the kitchen. "By the way, the next time you clean the kitchen, you might want to load the dishes in the dishwasher. It's easier." Smiling, he walked out the door.

His stomach growled, but he ignored it. He figured for some reason he just wasn't supposed to eat tonight.

After breakfast Lauren plopped down in a chair in the great room and spent much of her morning poring over the Internet, searching for job opportunities at various points in the country. By the time she decided to call it a day, her neck ached and the house was quiet. She had no idea where everyone had gone. Had she been that engrossed in what she was doing?

Gathering up the cord for her laptop, she felt just a little disappointed that everyone had left without her.

"Time for a break," Garrett said with a large grin, surprising her. He walked over with a tall glass of iced tea and placed it on the stand beside her. "I thought you might appreciate this."

This guy was something else. She'd like to wrap him up and cart him back to Indiana. Unfortunately, there was that whole faith thing still between them. "Thanks." She took a drink, then placed the glass back on the coaster. "Where did everyone go?"

Garrett thought a moment. "Hmm, let's see. Gracie went shopping, Nikki is at the bookstore, Billie is at the gun shop and Ellen is reading a book up in her room."

"Oh."

"Gracie and I are supposed to go back out, I think tomorrow night."

Lauren looked up. She wondered why he was telling her.

"I know I already took her out, but she very adamantly reminded me that we came home early the last time because I had a headache. She felt cheated." He rolled his eyes.

"You're taking Billie out tonight, aren't you?"

"Yeah. I might get to eat that steak that I couldn't eat in front of Nikki last night."

Lauren laughed.

Although Garrett didn't act all that interested in Gracie, Lauren couldn't deny the knot in her stomach at the thought of the two of them spending an evening together. After all, Gracie was beautiful—even charming when she worked at it. Before she could think on it further, her cell phone trilled.

"Excuse me," she said to Garrett. "Hello?"

"Lauren! How are you, girlfriend?" Candace's voice greeted her.

"Candace, hi!" She put her hand over the receiver. "I'm sorry, Garrett. I need to take this."

"No problem."

Lauren got up, walked to her room and closed the door.

"So tell me all about it. How are things going?"

"I'm having a wonderful time. It's been interesting, I will say that."

"Oh, I'm so glad. What do you think of the owners? Aren't they the nicest couple?"

Lauren was confused. "Well, actually, there is only one owner now. His wife died three years ago."

"What?"

"That's what he told me."

Silence.

"Candace?"

"Look, Lauren, I don't know what's going on, but I can assure you my aunt is very much alive."

"Your aunt?" Lauren had no clue what Candace could possibly be talking about.

"My aunt and uncle own the bed-and-breakfast."

"Well, I hate to break it to you, but there's been a buyout here. A widower owns it. You had to know that, since you set me up in this reality contest."

"Okay, now I'm totally confused. What are you talking about—reality contest?"

"Yeah, right, as if you don't know. The surprise, remember?"

"Listen, Lauren, now you're scaring me."

"I don't get it."

A pause. Then a sigh. "Look, Gwen and I set you up

at my aunt and uncle's bed-and-breakfast. Their son was to be home from traveling in Europe. We were hoping the two of you would meet and hit it off."

Lauren sat speechless.

"Are you okay, Lauren?"

"I—I don't know what to say. I'm at Woods Inn Bed and Breakfast and—"

"Woods Inn?"

"Huh? Oh, yeah."

"My aunt and uncle's B and B is called Woodwards' Bed and Breakfast."

"But this is on Pine Road."

"So is my aunt and uncle's."

"Oh, dear," Lauren said in defeat. "I've really messed things up."

"You know, my aunt and uncle called several times, but they didn't say anything on the answering machine, other than that they needed to talk to me." She hesitated. "I suppose they didn't want to worry me while I was traveling so far from home and couldn't do anything about it. I just tried to return their call, but they were out." She laughed. "Okay. This is too much! So tell me about this reality-contest thing. And how did you get by without paying for your stay?"

"You see, that's just it. The people here thought I was a contestant in this contest his daughters set up on the Internet. Something about 'Win Daddy's Heart.'"

Candace whistled. "Oh, my, this is way better than what we had planned."

"Now, cut that out, Candace. This is serious. I've

messed everything up. I feel horrible that you and Gwen paid for my way at your relatives' B and B and I didn't even show up."

Candace laughed. "Well, it's not a big deal, really. Auntie gave us a great rate. Besides, everything has turned out all right. Though I'm sure my cousin is disappointed." She laughed. "So tell me about this guy."

Lauren spent the next half hour talking about what had happened since she'd arrived at the B and B and telling her friend about Garrett.

"What is this guy's name again? Garrett what?"

"Cantrell."

"Cantrell? You don't mean it!"

"Yes, I do. Why? Do you know him?"

"I sure do! When Garrett got out of college, he worked for my dad. Dad sort of mentored him. Even helped him start his own business. He and Susie used to come to our house for dinner. Nice people. I had forgotten all about Susie's car accident. That's too bad."

"Yeah."

"Is he doing okay?"

"I think he's working through it. Still struggling some with the whys of it all."

"Oh. Garrett was a strong Christian man when I knew him."

"I think he's just confused right now. Kind of blaming God for everything. He still believes, but they're just not on speaking terms."

"Sounds as though you've gathered a lot of information there. So do you think you'll win?"

"Win what?"

"Daddy's heart."

Lauren almost choked. "I don't think so. Besides, we're too different."

"In what way?"

"Oh, I don't know. He enjoys small-town living, and I'm ready to spread my wings, for one thing."

"Well, Lauren, I don't know what he's told you, but he's anything but a small-town kind of guy. He loves to travel. Used to travel all the time. He settled down because that's what Susie wanted. Now, don't get me wrong. I think he does enjoy small-town living at Bliss Village. He probably tired of the constant frenzy his work brought about, but I also know he's quite capable of having a good time and seeing the world."

Lauren's heart blipped for a second. She couldn't believe what she was hearing from Candace. That was certainly a side of Garrett Cantrell she hadn't learned about yet.

"I don't know what your take is on him, Lauren, but I can assure you Garrett is a great guy. I know how much he loved the Lord when I knew him, and I'm sure he can't stay away from that for long. He just has to work through some things. My parents think the world of him. He has two wonderful daughters, too."

Somehow just hearing her friend's side of things made Lauren feel better about everything. Though she didn't know why. She would be leaving in less than a week.

"Hey, listen, Lauren, I'm late for an appointment, and I have to go. I'll call you back later and we'll talk some more, okay? And in the meantime, enjoy this guy. He's quite a catch! I have no doubt he'll get things sorted out with God."

"Thanks, Candace. Talk to you soon."

Lauren clicked off her cell phone and stared at it. Candace's words played back in her mind about Garrett being strong in the faith. That excited her, but it really didn't matter now. She'd have to go home. After all, she wasn't really a true contestant, nor had she ever been.

She only came on this adventure because her friends insisted, and they paid for it. But they paid another B and B. She couldn't ask for more help. She just wondered how she could pay for her stay up to this point, with no employment prospects.

Chapter Fifteen

Garrett stepped into the diner and spotted Paul Burke waving. He joined him at the booth.

"Hi, Paul," he said, extending his hand.

"Good to see you, Garrett." The guys shook hands and sat down. "So how have you been?"

"Doing all right," Garrett said, feeling a little nervous now that he was with Paul. Though he was a good friend, Paul had the eyes of a pastor. The kind that could see through to your soul.

"How are things with the bed-and-breakfast?"

"It's holding its own." He adjusted the watch on his wrist. "I have as much business as I want, really. We don't depend on the income so much, since I have my investments to provide what we need."

"Well, you've got an interesting group of guests there right now," Paul said with a vigorous laugh. "I'm struggling with that envy thing, you know."

Garrett looked up in surprise and grinned when he

saw the teasing in Paul's eyes. "Trust me, having a house full of women is not as good as it sounds."

Paul laughed again. "I suppose that's true enough."

Just then the server came and took their orders, saying she would be back in a moment with their drinks.

"I got such a kick out of it when Macy and Molly told me what they had done. I admit I wasn't sure how you would take to it." He rubbed his jaw and studied Garrett for a moment. "Seems to me you've handled it pretty well."

"What's a dad to do?" He intertwined his fingers in front of him and stared at them. "I mean, the girls went to all that trouble. They meant well, but I sure wish they had asked me first."

The server brought their soft drinks.

"So how are things going with the church?" Garrett asked before taking a drink.

"Going well. As you know, we've had quite a few members in the hospital lately, so I've been busy with visitation. Hopefully, they're all on the mend now."

"How long have you been at the church, Paul?"

"Mmm, let's see. It's been pretty close to six years."

Garrett shook his head. "Hard to believe."

A pause settled between them. Paul looked at Garrett. "It's been a while since we've gotten together. Makes me think there must be something in particular on your mind?"

Garrett swallowed. He wasn't sure he was ready for this. He blew out a sigh.

Paul waited patiently.

Garrett looked at his fingers again. "I've been doing

some thinking, and just wondered—" He looked up. "How do people get back on track?"

Paul's eyebrows pulled together. "Back on track?"

Garrett licked his lips and kept his eyes down. "I shut God out of my life when Susie died. I think you know that." He looked up at his friend.

Paul kept his gaze on Garrett but said nothing.

"Well, um, I still have lots of questions, things I don't understand. But, well, I don't want to live this way."

The server came with their lunches and placed them in front of each one. Paul said a prayer for their meal, then they started to eat.

"I think I understand what you mean, Garrett. You've been through a lot. What you've been through could shake the faith of the most ardent follower of Christ. God understands our questions, and He understands that we are mere men with little understanding of the eternal realm of things."

Garrett didn't say anything.

"Are you ready to get back on track, Garrett?"

He looked up at Paul. "That's just it. I'm not sure. I mean, I want to, but I don't know if I'm ready. There's still so much in the way." He hesitated. "Don't get me wrong. I believe in God. I'm just not sure what I think of Him right now."

"At least you're thinking of Him. Seems to me you're headed in the right direction."

Garrett looked at him.

"You wouldn't have bothered to set up this luncheon if God wasn't dealing with your heart."

Garrett hadn't thought of that.

"You see, regardless of how we treat Him, God doesn't give up on us."

Garrett felt a knot in his throat. "I guess I want you to pray for me. Pray that I will find my way back," he said almost in a whisper.

"You got it, buddy." He put his sandwich down. "And how about we take it a step further. Let's get together every Monday for lunch and touch base. I won't pressure you, but we can just talk about how things are going, and if you have any questions, I'll be here for you."

Garrett thought a moment. "Okay."

Lauren settled onto the bench in the woods. Dressed in a halter top, Nocchi lay down near Lauren's feet. Lauren could see why Garrett loved this place. There was something peaceful about it.

She took a deep breath and looked out into the trees. Hard to believe she had been there only a little over a week. It seemed a lifetime in many ways. She had grown to really care for Garrett, Macy and Molly. But by Saturday, she would walk out of their lives forever. Life could be hard sometimes.

Thoughts of Jeff and Camilla came to her. She really could make no sense of that whole mess. Why had Jeff pledged his love to her, only to toss it aside for someone he had known all his life? Could their relationship have been ongoing over the years? Lauren didn't think so. Why would they hide it? He could just as easily have asked Camilla to marry him. None of it made sense.

They must have recognized a spark between them after he and Lauren were engaged. Why didn't Camilla come and talk to her? Not that she would have taken it well. No matter how she analyzed the matter, it was painful.

She bowed her head.

Lord, I tell You my concerns about Garrett not following You, when I'm just as guilty of shutting You out. I've pushed aside my bitter and unforgiving spirit, all the while telling myself it wasn't there. But You knew. I have to let it go. Still, I know it will not be a one-time thing for me. I have a tendency to pick problems back up and clutch them tightly to my chest.

A draft of air rustled through the pines as Lauren sat in the quiet, hearing only the pounding of her heart.

I want to surrender it all to You. I want to be able to forgive Jeff and Camilla and to love them in spite of what they've done to me. You prayed for Your enemies and for those who spitefully used You.

Lauren felt a twinge. She couldn't even say that Jeff and Camilla were her enemies. In fact, they were not. That's why it hurt so much. She loved them. What surprised her most was she loved them still.

She heard a twig snap. Nocchi barked once. Lauren's eyes blinked open and she turned to see Garrett standing at the entrance of the woods, a short distance from her.

"I'm sorry. I didn't see that you were busy until I stepped closer." He turned to go.

"Don't go, Garrett." She decided she needed to tell him about the mix-up with the B and B.

He looked at her. "You sure?"

"I'm sure."

He sat down beside her on the bench. "I didn't know if you would see my note on the table downstairs when you finished with your phone call."

"I saw it. How was your lunch?"

"It was good. I met with my pastor."

Her heart gave a leap. "You did?"

"Yeah. I don't think I told you who I was meeting."

She shook her head.

"We had an interesting talk."

Lauren felt hopeful, but kept silent, hoping he would continue.

"I'm not where I need to be, but it's a start."

She thought of her own prayer, wanting to change her attitude toward Jeff and Camilla. It seemed God was working on both of them. "You're right, it is a start." They sat in silence for a moment. "Uh, Garrett, there's something I need to talk to you about."

"Yes?"

She looked at him. "Boy, I'm not sure where to begin."

"Is it that bad?"

"Well, it's a bit humbling, I'm afraid."

"Oh?"

She explained her conversation with Candace and how Lauren had gotten mixed up and arrived at the wrong bed-and-breakfast. She went on to tell him of her friends' true surprise and how Lauren had thought it was the reality contest.

Garrett scratched his temple. "I can see what you mean. That is some mix-up."

"Well, I just want you to know that since I'm not a true contestant, I'll pull out. And I will pay you for my stay here as soon as I get another job. In the meantime, could I make payments?"

He held up his hands. "Whoa. Please don't tell me you're pulling out. You can't possibly leave me alone with those other four." He grinned, causing her to relax. "And I won't hear of you paying. I've more than enjoyed having you here. You're the only one who has made this bearable. I mean, the other ladies are nice and all, but well, I'm afraid it would have been uncomfortable for all of us."

"I don't know, Garrett. I feel funny about this. It doesn't seem right."

"I'll tell you what. We'll talk it over with Macy and Molly. They set this contest up. If they agree with me, you stay, all right? They're the ones who set the rules, so they can decide whatever they want." He searched her face. "Is it a deal?"

She thought a moment. "Okay," she said with some reluctance, though she still felt a little concerned.

"Great. Speaking of which, I think Macy and Molly got home a little while ago. You want to go talk to them now?"

"Sure."

They headed back to the house with Nocchi trotting happily alongside them.

Garrett and Lauren entered the back door and walked in through the kitchen, dining area. She was laughing as she told him a story that one of her colleagues had shared with her. Once they reached the hallway, Garrett came to a dead halt. Lauren looked up to see Macy standing at the front door with Drew Huntington.

"Hi, Daddy," she said rather nervously. "Drew stopped by to invite me to dinner." Her expression held a mix of defiance and a child's plea.

Lauren held her breath, sure that a battle was coming. She and Macy shared a glance.

Drew shifted from one leg to another and looked at Garrett.

"I tell you what, Drew. How about you join us for dinner tonight? We want to get to know you a little more."

Macy's eyes grew wide. She turned to Drew.

"Um, sure thing, Mr. Cantrell. That would be great."

"You can come here around six-thirty."

Drew looked at Macy and then back to Garrett. "Okay, uh, I'll see you all then." He looked back at Macy and grinned before walking out the door.

Lauren wasn't sure how Macy would feel about the outcome, but before Lauren could leave the scene, Macy turned back around to face Garrett.

"Thanks, Dad," she said before walking past them and going up the stairs.

Lauren slowly let out her breath. Her gaze locked with Garrett's.

"I think that went rather well. How about you?" He grinned and winked at Lauren.

She smiled.

He scratched his head. "Course, now I'll have to reschedule my date with Billie. I'm wondering if I'll ever get to eat that steak." He laughed.

Lauren chuckled with him. There was something special about this man.

Yes, something very special indeed.

By the time Drew returned, Garrett and all the contestants were there, Macy and Molly had arranged the table settings and dinner was ready to be served.

"Come on in," Macy said, motioning for Drew to find his seat at the table.

He was dressed in a short-sleeve blue-and-black striped polo shirt with khaki pants. Lauren glanced at Macy and noticed she looked equally nice in green canvas capris and a white tee.

"I hope you can eat grilled lake trout," Molly said, placing on the dining table a large serving dish with the main entrée.

"Wow, looks great," Drew said, appearing quite impressed.

Lauren couldn't help but beam at the young couple. Once everyone was seated, Garrett asked Lauren to say the prayer, which surprised her, though she was happy to do so. After prayer, they began to pass the bowls of food around the table.

"So, how's the reporting business these days?" Garrett asked, scooping a large helping of mashed potatoes onto his plate.

"It's going well. Never dull, that's for sure," Drew said, quickly glancing at Macy as if to make sure he was doing okay with her dad.

"I just don't know how you get your little ol' self in front of that camera and talk away. Why, I would freeze up on the very spot," Gracie said, batting her eyelashes ever so sweetly.

Drew shrugged. "You get used to it."

The smell of dinner mingled with the clank of silverware as the little group concentrated on their meal rather than talking, for the moment.

"These sautéed vegetables are wonderful, Macy and Molly," Lauren said, smiling at them.

"Thanks," Molly said. "We used a special seasoning."

"Would you pass the salad, please?" Billie said to

Ellen. "You know, I remember a time when I couldn't eat fish. But then I learned how healthy it was, and I've been eating it ever since. Plus, I love to go fishing, so I figured I'd better eat 'em if I'm going to catch 'em." She tore off a hunk of roll and shoved it into her mouth.

Lauren noticed Nikki had a special salad made just for her, minus the meat.

"Um, I don't eat a lot of fish, but, um, I think this is, um, good," Ellen managed. Everyone at the table looked at her. It was the most words she had uttered at one time since she'd arrived at the bed-and-breakfast.

"Thanks, Ellen," Molly and Macy said in unison.

Gracie took a drink, then turned to Drew. "I think I'm the only one who got to see the clip. Mr. Huntington, I must say you did a great job with that little news story of our contest. Though I wish your cameraman had not taken a profile shot of me. I never look good from that view." She pretended to pout.

Drew stopped chewing and looked at her. "Huh? Oh, sorry."

"You know, I never did see that on the news," Garrett said, taking a bite of the lemon-flavored fish.

Drew looked up. "Really? Well, I can get you a video copy if you want one."

"Thanks."

Lauren noticed the look of pleasure on Macy's face and felt happy for her. From what Lauren could see, this was the most Macy and Garrett had gotten along in the same room since Lauren had arrived there.

"Oh, I forgot to tell you guys," Drew said, wiping his mouth on the cloth napkin. "This is really exciting. I can't believe I haven't mentioned it before now."

Everyone looked at him.

"Just like I predicted earlier, that little news piece has been picked up by the big guys."

Lauren's glance darted to Garrett. The color drained from his face.

"What does that mean?" Garrett squeaked. He cleared his throat.

"Oh, it's good. It will make you famous. Give you more business than you'll know what to do with." Drew sat back in his chair puffed up like a proud rooster.

"Not to mention how it helps your career along," Garrett said with a definite edge to his voice.

Uh-oh, this conversation was taking a turn south.

Macy looked to Lauren for help. Lauren shrugged ever so slightly.

"People from all over the country will see that clip. It's quite ingenious what your girls have done, really." Drew looked at Macy and winked.

Garrett glared at "his girls."

"Is anyone ready for dessert?" Molly asked, already rising from her chair.

"We aren't finished with our meal yet, Molly," Garrett said through clenched teeth.

She sat back down.

"Well, ain't that something?" Gracie joined in. "We'll all be on television across the nation. Imagine that."

"Yeah, no doubt we'll get plenty of mail at the station from secret admirers once they all get a look at you ladies," Drew said in an obvious attempt to ease the tension.

"Really?" Gracie's voice was practically breathless, as if she might hyperventilate or something.

"Sure." Drew rubbed the back of his neck.

Ellen shoveled food nervously into her mouth.

Billie seemed to have ignored the conversation altogether.

Nikki finished her salad and started on her vegetables. "I can't remember much about the interview. Did you tell anything about us?"

"Sure I did," Drew encouraged. "I said a little blurb about each one of you. Let's see, I mentioned that you were a vegetarian," he said to Nikki.

Her lips curled upward and she sat up straighter in her chair.

Garrett let out a quiet groan, but Lauren heard him.

"I told them that you were from Tennessee," he said to Gracie, who blushed on cue.

He turned to Lauren. "And I think I mentioned the fact that you were recently set free from the jerk to whom you had been engaged. Well, maybe not in exactly those words, but close."

Lauren had just taken a sip of iced tea, and immediately choked on it. Garrett slapped her on the back so many times that she wanted to slug him. When she finally caught her breath, everyone stared at her.

"Are you all right?" Drew asked. "I hope I didn't cause that."

Lauren looked at the worry lines on Macy's face. "Uh, no, no, my tea just went down the wrong way," she said in a raspy voice.

Macy visibly relaxed.

Lauren wondered if her parents might have seen the clip from their home in Florida.

Their discussion moved on from there to the best

fishing in the area, but the words blurred around Lauren as the other thoughts hit her. Drew had mentioned her ex-fiancé? How had he known about that? And what if Jeff or Camilla saw it? The knot in Lauren's stomach grew. She hadn't given the details of their split to distant friends and family. She figured it was enough that the wedding was called off, without going into the gory details. Besides, no one appreciated being rejected. How could she survive this humiliation?

"Lauren, are you all right?"

She turned to see the concern on Garrett's face. "You know, I'm not feeling very well."

"I hope it wasn't the fish," Molly said.

"Oh no, no, it wasn't the fish. I'm sure I'll be fine. But if you wouldn't mind, I think I'll go to my room for a little while."

"Sure, do what you have to do," Garrett said, pulling out her chair so she could stand.

"I do so hope you're not coming down with something, Lucy," Gracie called after her.

If Lauren had had the strength, she would have whacked her on the way out, but she didn't. And then there was that whole prayer thing earlier that afternoon….

Chapter Sixteen

Lauren paced in her room a little while, trying to figure out how to get through the latest catastrophe. "Just breathe, Lauren," she told herself, finally settling onto the edge of her bed. She took some deep breaths and tried to calm down.

Someone knocked at the door.

"Yes?"

"Lauren, it's Macy. May I come in?"

Lauren took another deep breath for good measure, got up and walked over to open the door.

"Come on in," Lauren said, closing the door behind Macy. They both sat on the bed.

"I'm sorry, Lauren, about what happened downstairs. I know what Drew said about your ex-fiancé upset you, and I don't blame you. But I wanted you to know that I did not tell him about our conversation. I have no idea how he knew that you had been engaged previously. I mean, I know when he interviewed you all, Gracie told him you were on the rebound, but no one said anything about your engagement."

Macy's eyes held an earnest gleam. Lauren believed her.

"Well, I just wanted you to know that I didn't tell him. I tried to get him to tell me how he found out, but he said he's not allowed to reveal his sources."

Lauren put her hand on Macy's. "It's all right, Macy. I mean, I'm a little embarrassed by it, but I doubt that many people I know will see the news clip. It's not really a big deal."

Macy gave a sigh of relief. "Thanks, Lauren." She rose from the bed when a knock sounded at the door. Lauren and Macy shared a glance.

"Come in."

The door opened and Molly entered, then closed the door.

"I thought I might find you here," she said, looking at Macy. She turned to Lauren. "I didn't know about the fiancé, Lauren, just in case you're wondering, so I didn't want you to think I had anything to do with Drew finding out."

"It's okay, Molly. Thanks."

"Well, we'll leave you alone," Macy said, joining Molly, who was turning back to the door.

"Oh, before you go—"

They turned to Lauren.

"Um, could you sit down for a minute?" She figured she might as well get everything over at one time.

Looking as though they were in trouble, they obediently walked over to the bed and sat down.

"It's not that bad," Lauren assured them. *At least not*

for you, she wanted to say, but didn't. Once they sat down, she told them all the circumstances around her arrival at the bed-and-breakfast, the whole mix-up and how she was not a true contestant. "I've told you all that because technically I'm not really a contestant and have basically been lodging here free without just cause."

"Oh, is that all?" Molly asked. "Good grief, I thought something was really wrong." She waved her hand to ignore the whole thing. "You're the only reason Dad hasn't disowned us yet. You *have* to stay. By showing up, you made yourself a contestant." Molly turned to Macy. "Isn't that right?"

"Absolutely. There's no turning back now. You got yourself into this, and you have to see it through to the end."

Lauren's heart warmed. "You know, you're going to have to come visit me in Indiana," she said with a grin.

They both brightened. "That would be awesome, Lauren," Macy said.

"And we can keep in touch through e-mail," Molly added.

"Absolutely. You know how a girl needs her computer." Lauren laughed.

The girls joined in. Then all grew quiet.

"Thanks, girls. For everything."

They looked at her. Macy reached for Lauren's arm. "You're welcome. Thank you for coming. I believe God sent you to us. I feel better when you're around, Lauren."

"Me, too," Molly said. "And anyone with half a brain can tell Dad does, too." She winked.

Lauren laughed again. "Okay, you two—" she edged them toward the door "—you behave yourselves."

"That's no fun," Molly said as she stepped out the door.

Lauren pretended to give her a swift kick on the way out. She closed the door and walked back over to the bed. She still didn't know how Drew had found out. She supposed that was a news reporter's job, to snoop until he found the truth. But no one knew except Macy and Garrett. He surely wouldn't have told Drew. He was hardly on speaking terms with the young reporter, and Garrett was not really the kind of guy who would pass along that kind of information. She appreciated that about him. Didn't blab everything, but rather respected people's privacy.

She sat a while longer, then it hit her. The night she had told Macy about Jeff, someone had come up behind them, interrupting their conversation. That person could have overheard and told Drew. That person?

Gracie Skinner.

Everyone scattered after dinner. Drew left early because he had an appointment. Macy and Molly disappeared soon after Lauren left the room. Garrett stacked the dishes in the dishwasher and turned it on. Some of the ladies had gone to their rooms, others settled in the great room. Garrett was headed for the den when he looked up the stairway and saw Macy leaving Lauren's room.

"Hey, Macy, will you meet me in the den, please?" he called up to her.

"Yeah."

He walked into the den and left the door open for her. She entered not too far behind.

"Close the door, please," he said.

Macy closed it, walked over to a chair and sat down. "What's up?"

"Well, I noticed you leaving Lauren's room, and I just wanted to make sure she was okay."

Macy had a soft expression on her face. She could see right through him and he knew it. He had to be careful. He didn't want to make it obvious to those around him that his feelings for Lauren were growing. They still had some things to work through—not to mention the fact they'd known each other only a little over a week.

"She's fine, Dad."

"Good." He sat down in a chair across from Macy. "Drew's announcement came as quite a blow to her, I think."

"Yeah."

"I wonder how he knew about it." Garrett rubbed his jaw.

"I have no idea. That's what bothered me. I didn't want Lauren to think I told him."

"Why would she think that?"

Macy looked at the floor. "Well, because one night we were talking and she told me about Jeff—her fiancé."

Garrett couldn't hide his surprise. Lauren had confided in Macy. Though the information surprised him, it also touched him. Lauren really seemed to care about his girls.

"I see. I suppose time will tell." Garrett fidgeted with his watch. "She probably still cares a lot about the guy. That's why she got all choked up." He was fishing for information, and by the look on Macy's face, he knew she could tell that's what he was up to.

She gave a knowing grin. "We didn't get that far."

He smirked. "Can't blame a guy for trying."

Macy chuckled.

Wait. Were they actually having a father/daughter moment? A bonding time here? This felt good to him. Really good. He didn't want to break the spell.

"Listen, Macy—"

She straightened in her chair, as though bracing herself against something.

"Uh, never mind."

She relaxed.

"Well, I guess I just wanted to make sure Lauren was doing okay."

"She's fine, Dad. Oh, one more thing. She told us about the mix-up with the B and B. Molly and I told her it was fine, and we still wanted her to stay on as a contestant. Hope that was okay."

"That's fine. I had hoped you would tell her that. In fact, I was sure you would."

She rose from her chair. With her hand on the doorknob, she turned back to Garrett. "I don't think she cares about that guy anymore, Dad. I think she's trying to move on with her life. She didn't actually tell me that—it's just one of those intuition things."

He studied his firstborn a moment. She was maturing, stretching, growing. Images of a child Macy flashed in his mind. Where had the days gone? He sure missed them, but for now he was thankful they had had a real conversation without it ending in an argument. "Thanks, Mace."

"Good night, Dad."

"Lauren, how you doing?" Gwen's voice came through the cell phone.

"Gwen, hi! So good to hear from you!" Lauren

kicked off her shoes and lay back on top of her bed. She could smell the cinnamon potpourri on a nearby stand.

"Hey, I had to hear how my friend's vacation was going. Getting any rest?" Gwen laughed good-naturedly. "Especially with the big mix-up?"

Lauren couldn't help but smile. "Yes, but it's definitely been an adventure."

"Okay, Lauren. Give the details."

Lauren adjusted the pillow behind her head and proceeded to tell Gwen everything about her being at the wrong bed-and-breakfast and how it had come about.

"Wow! We had good intentions, but it sounds to me as though God had other plans for you," Gwen said with a perky voice.

"Well, I don't know that He had anything to do with it." She plopped her right leg over her left one, crossing them at the feet.

"Oh, phooey," Gwen said. "You know He's involved in every aspect of our lives. It will be interesting to see how this all shakes out."

"Well, I don't know what you mean, Gwen."

"I mean, you, Daddy's heart and all that."

Lauren shook her head. Gwen, ever the bubbling romantic.

"Hey, listen, Lauren, there's another reason I'm calling, actually."

Uh-oh. Something in Gwen's voice didn't sit well with Lauren. It had lost its perk. "Oh?" She propped herself up on her elbows.

"Um, yeah." She hesitated. "I went to the store last night, and who do you suppose I ran into?" Lauren could tell Gwen was trying to sound happy here.

"I don't know, Gwen, but I have a feeling you're about to tell me," Lauren teased, trying to calm her jumpy nerves.

"Well, I was in the produce department. I had this insatiable craving for taco salad, you know, and so I was picking up a head of lettuce. By the way, I have the best recipe for taco salad—have I shared that with you?"

Lauren sighed. "No—yes—no...I don't know, Gwen. Who did you see?" She didn't mean to be impatient, but good grief, Gwen could try the patience of Job.

"Oh, yeah. Sorry. Uh, I saw Jeff...." Her voice trailed off with his name, making it almost too soft to hear.

"Did you say you saw Jeff?"

"Yes."

"As in Levinger?"

"The very same."

Lauren waited a moment to digest the information. "That's nice. How was he?" she asked, trying to sound nonchalant.

"Well, that's the strange part. He, uh, asked how you were enjoying your stay at the bed-and-breakfast, and said he couldn't remember the name of the town, but he had heard it was a really nice place. Said he'd like to visit it sometime, wanted to know if I knew the name of the town."

Lauren felt a hot rush surge through her. She swallowed hard and fast. "What did you tell him, Gwen?"

"Well, he caught me off guard."

Lauren groaned. "You didn't."

"I told him it was where we always met for our gatherings in Bliss Village."

Lauren fell back against the pillow. She could feel a headache coming on.

"Well, he put me on the spot, and I didn't have time to think. I'm sorry, Lauren."

Lauren blew out a sigh. "No, no, it's all right, Gwen. It's a long story." Her mind raced. Okay, so he had seen the news clip. What did that matter? Why did he want to know where she was staying? Had something upset him in the clip? She needed to see that video.

"Lauren, are you still there?"

"I'm here."

"Listen, I hope he won't bother you or anything." Gwen's voice sounded uncertain and upset.

"Don't worry about it, Gwen. It's probably nothing."

"Okay." She perked up again. "Well, I just thought I would call and see how you were doing, and also let you know about that in case it was something you needed to know."

"Okay. Thanks, Gwen."

"I can't wait to hear on Saturday if you've won Daddy's heart."

Lauren forced a chuckle. "Yeah, you'll be one of the first to know if that happens."

"I'll talk to you later, okay, Lauren?"

"Yeah. See you soon." Lauren clicked off the phone and dropped it beside her on the bed. She had to see that video. Since Macy would know how to get hold of Drew, Lauren stepped out her bedroom door to see if Macy was home. She finally found Macy downstairs in the kitchen.

"Hey, Macy. Do you know how I could get in touch with Drew?"

Macy turned off the iced-tea maker and looked at Lauren. "Sure. Everything okay?"

"Yeah, it's fine. I was just kind of curious to see that video, and I wondered when he was going to deliver it."

"Oh, I can tell you that. He's dropping it by tomorrow morning on his way to work. Probably around seven-thirty."

"Will we still be here?"

"Oh, yeah. We won't leave until probably around ten o'clock."

"Super. Thanks, Macy." Seven-thirty. With the bike ride and picnic Garrett had scheduled for tomorrow, Lauren figured they would have a full day. If Macy was right, she'd be able to see the video before they left.

She could only hope that it wouldn't ruin her day.

Chapter Seventeen

Lauren was showered, dressed and downstairs eating breakfast by the time Drew arrived the next morning. Macy answered the door. Trying not to appear too excited with the prospect of watching the video, Lauren continued to eat her eggs and attempted to ignore the butterflies in her stomach. She had made it through her eggs and a piece of toast before Macy and Drew entered the kitchen. She worried when she caught a glimpse of the expression on Drew's face.

"Good morning, ladies." He turned to Garrett. "Morning, sir."

Garrett grunted.

The women turned to him and exchanged pleasantries.

He scratched his head. "I'm sorry to say I won't be able to show you the video. It seems we had some mechanical problems that night and were unable to get the program taped. I'm sorry."

The other contestants looked only mildly interested. Lauren had hoped the tape would give her some insight as to why Jeff would be seeking her whereabouts. Oh, well, it wasn't the end of the world. So what if he knew she was at a bed-and-breakfast in some reality contest? He could see that she wasn't afraid of adventure anymore. The rumbling in her stomach quieted a little. Everything would be all right.

"Thanks for letting us know, Drew," Garrett finally said. "We're probably better off not seeing ourselves on TV anyway."

"They say television adds ten pounds," Gracie said. "I'm sure glad it didn't do that to me." She smoothed her hair and batted her eyelashes at Garrett.

It's all about you, isn't it, Gracie? Lauren wanted to say, but then that would be giving her tongue free rein and she knew the Bible had something to say about that. Instead, she swallowed the words with her last bite of toast.

"Well, I'd better get to work. Thanks for understanding," Drew said. He waved goodbye, and Macy walked him to the door.

"Once you all are finished with breakfast," Garrett said to the ladies, "we'll meet around back. I have the bikes and helmets out and ready to go."

Nikki, Billie and Lauren all looked up from the table and nodded. Ellen looked up, but held perfectly still—all except for her glasses shifting on her nose a little.

With a sharp turn, Gracie whirled around to face Garrett. "We have to wear helmets?" she practically shrieked.

He looked at her much the same way as an impatient teacher would view a tiresome student. "Yes, Gracie, you have to wear a helmet."

"But my hair." She stroked it. With a pout she glanced at the others, then back at Garrett. "I got up early to work on it so it would look nice. A helmet will make it look like a dented marshmallow."

Snickers rippled around the table.

"I think your safety is a bit more important than your hair, Gracie." Garrett turned on his heels and headed out the back door, dismissing the matter entirely.

Gracie's sweet little ol' pout turned to a scowl. "I don't know why we have to wear stupid helmets." She placed her bowl on the table with a thud and poured some cereal into it. The others watched her. She looked up. "What?" Gracie's face twisted from pretty to ugly in a matter of seconds. Lauren wished Garrett could see the Southern beauty now.

After breakfast Lauren took care of Nocchi's needs, then joined the others outside in the back. Garrett discussed the general area of where they would be traveling and the type of terrain over which they would go biking.

Garrett looked overhead. "The sky is a perfect blue and the weatherman is promising sunshine all day. Since we won't be up in the high mountains, we should be okay. The important thing is that we all stay together. I'll lead the way, and I want you all to bike behind me in single file. We'll fall in line here and stay that way for the duration. Though we'll travel at a decent pace, I will tone it down somewhat for those of you who may not be used to the exercise."

Billie snickered.

"It's not an endurance race. I hope we have a good

time. After our trip we'll stop at a park, eat a picnic lunch by the lake, then bike our way back home."

Nearby, Bear whined and paced back and forth in front of his doghouse.

"Bear, settle down. I'll take you for a walk when I get back," Garrett said. The dog immediately sat back on his haunches and let out an enormous yawn. "Obviously you can hardly wait."

The women laughed.

Garrett turned back to the contestants. "Everyone ready to go?"

They nodded.

"I'll go tell Macy and Molly when to meet us at the picnic site with the goods." He winked and stepped inside the house.

Lauren took a deep breath of the morning air and adjusted the water bottle in her backpack. Gracie grumbled and Lauren looked over to see her fussing with her helmet. No doubt she'd rather be putting on a crown. Lauren's gaze flitted to Billie. She, on the other hand, thrived on this type of adventure. Billie's face positively glowed.

Garrett stepped back outside. "Okay, let's get started." He strapped on his helmet and climbed onto his bike. Everyone fell into line behind him. He looked back and waved his arm forward.

They were off and pedaling.

With the cool air brushing against her face, Lauren felt thankful they had started on their journey early in the day. Sheltered from the day's heat by the shade of the pine woods, Lauren thought this little excursion just might be fun after all. There was little opportunity to visit with one another since they were traveling in single file, but it gave Lauren time to think about her plans after she left the bed-and-breakfast on Saturday.

Hard to believe this would all be over so soon. She had to admit the whole adventure had turned out much better than she had anticipated. What would have happened had she gone to the other bed-and-breakfast? Candace had called again and said her cousin was still in Europe. So indeed Lauren would have stayed at the other bed-and-breakfast and truly rested. With the stretch in her leg muscles just now the rest idea didn't sound all that bad, but still she was glad she had made the mistake of going to Garrett's place instead.

She looked up at him. Not wanting to assert herself, she had stumbled into line behind Garrett and two others. Nikki was directly behind him, Ellen behind Nikki, then Lauren, Gracie and Billie. Lauren was amused that Billie had insisted on being the last person in line. She evidently perceived it her duty to make sure everyone stayed in line and obeyed orders. The woman should have been a marine sergeant.

Garrett's body took the form of a professional biker. He leaned into his bike, legs taut, arms strong for the task. His brown T-shirt pulled tight across his back, revealing strong, corded muscles. Anyone could see that he took good care of himself.

Lauren thought Garrett Cantrell a puzzle. Why did he keep himself holed up at the bed-and-breakfast? At least, that's what Macy and Molly basically had told her. He didn't hang out with other guys, didn't date, pretty much stayed at home, made repairs on the B and B, fathered the girls and that was it.

The whole idea saddened Lauren. He had too much life in him to give up so easily. She thought of her own situation since the split from Jeff. Hadn't she done the same thing? She chased the annoying thought away.

She knew Garrett still hurt from his wife's death. His love for her seemed to go beyond the grave, and he didn't appear willing to let her go. Lauren thought a moment about how hard it would be to become the wife of a widower—especially one who couldn't let go of his first wife. She mentally shook her head. That would be a miserable existence, she felt quite sure.

After a while Garrett waved his hand, motioning for everyone to stop behind him. They pulled over to a small clearing on the right, near a fallen pine tree. A cracked trunk spiked upward. They took care not to get too close for fear someone could fall against it and get stabbed by the splintered wood.

Garrett pulled off his helmet, and everyone else did the same.

"I thought now would be a good time to stop and take a break." He turned and pulled the water bottle from his pack and took a swig.

Without saying a word, the ladies yanked on their packs and pulled out their own bottles. After drinking his fill, Garrett swiped his mouth with the back of his hand.

"So what do you think? Are you having a good time?" Garrett's skin looked vibrant, his eyes bright and shining.

Lauren and a couple of others said, "Yes."

Ellen and Gracie said nothing. They sat in the shade of the forest taking time to catch their breath and cool off after their drink. Gracie fidgeted some more with her helmet. Ellen adjusted her glasses.

"We'll be there shortly." He checked his watch. "We're making good time. Macy and Molly will be at the site with lunch in about half an hour. We should get there close to that." He looked at the group. "Everyone ready?" When no one complained, he tipped his head. "Great, let's go."

They pedaled farther, and this last stretch seemed harder than the first. The sun had penetrated through the thick of the forest, warming the already overheated bikers, and slowing their pace.

"We'll stop just beyond that hill," Garrett yelled over his shoulder as he pointed ahead.

Lauren's leg muscles had started to burn. She hadn't considered herself out of shape until she came on this trip. Once she got back to Indiana, she was going to have to increase her workout intensity.

She pumped up the hill, causing her legs to burn all the more. Not wanting to lose her momentum, she pedaled harder. Her breath grew shallow, and her heart thumped wildly against her chest. Just as they crested the top, she breathed a sigh of relief to see the downhill slope, knowing they would coast, if only for a moment, before they reached the beach just beyond the highway at the end of the stretch.

Garrett and Nikki started down, then Ellen and Lauren. Just as Lauren started to relax and enjoy the descent, someone behind her screamed and the next thing she knew, Gracie flew by her at breakneck speed. It appeared her brakes weren't working. The horror on Gracie's face let them all know she was in trouble. Gracie was past Garrett before he could react and he took off after her. Lauren could barely breathe. He had to get to Gracie before she reached the highway.

Oh, God, please help them. Stop Gracie in time. Please, God, don't let anything happen to either one of them.

The morning wind dried the tears on Lauren's cheeks as she pedaled downward, struggling all the way to dodge protruding tree branches, pinecones, leaves and bark debris on the path. She continued to pray as panic surged through every inch of her, causing her to tingle and feel slightly light-headed.

Skidding to a halt, Lauren reached the bottom of the hill in time to see Garrett and Gracie racing across the highway. The other bikes sprayed dirt as they stopped next to Lauren. Everyone watched in horror, no one saying a word.

Car horns blared. Tires screeched. Garrett and Gracie darted across the endless pavement like manipulated characters in a video game. This couldn't be real.

A semi headed straight toward them. Its screaming horn split the air in a blast of noise. Garrett pedaled for his life. Gracie's fingers pumped the faulty handbrakes of the bike that held her captive, but they refused to work.

Sweat beaded upon Lauren's head. *Please, God.*

Ellen screamed. Billie gasped.

The semi crossed a lane, missing the bikers by a thread. Garrett plowed into Gracie's bike. The metal tangled, causing them to spill upon the sandy beach at the other side.

When the way was clear, Lauren and the others crossed the highway. They dropped their bikes and ran to Gracie, who lay still on the beach, her leg swollen and bruised. Her face was smudged with dirt and sand. Fringes of hair lay limp beneath her helmet. An ugly gash stretched across her left leg, undoubtedly where Garrett had run into her. He pulled off his helmet and sat close to her head, stroking her arm, offering words of encouragement.

"Dad!" Macy and Molly shouted as they ran toward Garrett. They were crying uncontrollably.

"I'm all right, girls. Everything is going to be okay."

They stopped short upon seeing Gracie on the ground and Garrett beside her.

Gracie tried to get up.

"No, stay down," Garrett said.

"But I need to get up. Help me. Somebody help me."

"You've hurt your leg, Gracie," Garrett warned.

"Has anyone called the ambulance?" Macy wanted to know.

Lauren wished she had brought her cell phone along.

A woman ran up behind them, quite out of breath. "I've called 9-1-1 and help is on the way."

"Anyone have a blanket or something to cover her with?" Garrett called out.

"I've got one in the car," another lady said, dashing toward the parking lot.

Once she returned with the blanket, Garrett covered Gracie with it.

The smattering of people who had been on the beach gathered near, some out of curiosity, others to see if they could help.

"Are you all right, sir?" someone said from the gradually forming crowd.

Garrett lifted dazed eyes. He had a cut on his cheek, his right arm was scratched and an ugly bruise swelled on the side of his right leg. "I'm fine."

Lauren trembled. She had never witnessed a near catastrophe before. What if Gracie had internal injuries? What if she wasn't going to be all right? Suddenly Lauren felt sick about her behavior toward Gracie. Even though most of her sarcasm had been inward, God knew she had said those things. Her eyes stung. She saw Ellen crying. Without a thought, Lauren walked over and put her arm around Ellen to console her. Billie and Nikki joined them on either side, arms around one another, no one saying a word. Lauren had never felt closer to any friends than she felt to those women at that moment. Funny how trauma could do that—make you see the worth of another in a real and different way than you had seen before.

"Am I going to be okay?" Gracie asked Garrett.

"You'll be just fine," he said with assurance. Lauren prayed he was right.

Gracie appeared satisfied with his answer, then glanced at Garrett once more. "Hey, how come you get to have your helmet off, and I still have to wear mine?" she managed to ask with a teasing lilt in her voice.

Everyone seemed to relax a little. Lauren felt the tension lift slightly.

Garrett said nothing as he continued to stroke Gracie's arm in a smooth rhythm. He looked up when the sirens sounded in the distance. Everyone turned to look as the noise got closer.

"They're coming for me, aren't they?" Gracie asked. She tightened her soiled hand around a cut on Garrett's wrist, causing him to wince. "Please don't leave me."

"I won't leave you, Gracie." With his fingers he brushed the hair away from her eyes.

Something about the tenderness in his voice, the look in his eyes as he watched Gracie, the way his rough hand soothed her arm with gentle strokes, all made Lauren turn away. She ached for Gracie and wanted with everything in her for Gracie to be okay, yet seeing Garrett look at another woman that way… How could she think of her own selfish feelings at a time such as this? Reining in her thoughts, she once again prayed for Gracie and Garrett and for God to help them all through this ordeal.

Garrett looked at his girls. "Can you get the others home for me?"

Molly was still crying.

"Yeah. Then can we come to the hospital?" Macy asked.

He thought a moment. "Yeah, I guess that's okay."

The ambulance pulled up and the EMTs jumped out of the emergency vehicle and headed their way with a stretcher.

Garrett closed his eyes as he sat on the bench inside the ambulance. One of the workers took Garrett's blood pressure while another man checked vitals on Gracie.

While the ambulance raced toward the hospital, Macy's and Molly's images burned in Garrett's mind. What if he had been hit by that semi that had careened toward them, missing them by mere inches? His girls would be alone. Worse than that, he wasn't ready to meet God. Garrett had turned his back on God. True, Garrett was attempting to get his life back in order, but he realized in that moment that it wasn't anything he could do on his own. He had to ask God to help him.

Up to this point, he'd had too much pride to ask God for anything. He didn't want to grovel again the way he had right before Susie died.

He could have died today. But for reasons he couldn't explain, God had spared him—given him another chance.

Why hadn't Susie gotten another chance? He shook himself. He couldn't change things. Besides, Susie had been ready to meet her Lord.

But Garrett? He knew the answer, though he didn't want to think about it. Still, he couldn't ignore that he had been given a second chance. Now it was up to him to do something with it. He could stay bitter, ruin his life and possibly poison the girls' lives as well, or he could make a new life for all of them, a God-centered life—not just one where they went to church together, but a home where Christ was the silent listener to every conversation, the unseen guest at every meal. He needed to make a choice. It sounded like a no-brainer, so what held him back?

He didn't have time to think about it. The ambulance came to a squalling halt and within seconds the back doors flew open.

Chapter Eighteen

By the time Gracie and Garrett arrived back at the bed-and-breakfast, everyone was waiting with open arms.

Garrett held the doors open for Gracie as she clumsily edged through the door on her new crutches. She told everyone she was fine and had just a small fracture.

Everyone squealed and ran over to help their two wounded friends. Molly brought out the popcorn and soft drinks while Macy helped her dad and Gracie get settled into chairs in the great room.

"Boy, this is a whole lot nicer than being at that hospital," Garrett said with a chuckle.

Dark circles shadowed his eyes. Bruises glared in the lamplight. Lauren noticed he moved gingerly on his chair as if to get comfortable.

"Well, I can tell you, that's the most exciting bike ride I've ever taken," Gracie said good-naturedly, surprising everyone with her humor.

"I don't think it was supposed to be quite that exciting," Nikki said.

"You got that right," Billie added. "We're just glad you're all right."

Lauren noticed Billie's words held sincerity, a certain vulnerability not normally found in her.

Ellen pushed her glasses back up her nose. "Um, we're glad you're both all right," she said with a blush.

"Thank you, Ellen," Gracie said with a genuine smile.

"Thanks," Garrett joined in.

Garrett and Gracie shared a glance, a look that said the near accident had affected them both in a real way and had drawn them closer together. Lauren suddenly felt as though she was on the outside looking in. Just what she was witnessing she didn't know.

"I'm sorry about your leg, Gracie, and I'm glad you're okay," Lauren managed. It was true, of course, but she struggled with whatever seemed to be happening between Gracie and Garrett.

"Thanks, Lauren. I really appreciate your concern."

And by the look on Gracie's face, Lauren was sure Gracie meant it.

The little group talked a while longer about the bicycling incident and the hospital visit. They decided they'd had enough adventure to last them for a while, and they would merely enjoy the scenery of Bliss Village for the remainder of their stay.

"Well, I don't know about you, but I'm bushed. I'm going to call it a night," Billie announced.

Others soon followed suit and everyone made their way to their rooms.

"Gracie, I'll be glad to help you to your room," Garrett offered.

Lauren swallowed hard as she watched the two of them share another glance.

"Why, thank you, Garrett," Gracie said, smiling ever so sweetly. Her smile seemed sincere this time, not dripping with hypocrisy as in past days. "But first I want to talk to Lauren a second, if you don't mind."

Oh, sure, she wanted to gloat. She had won Daddy's heart, and she wanted to rub it in Lauren's face. Wait a minute, Lauren thought. This woman has just been through something pretty traumatic. Give her a chance. Still, not knowing what Gracie might say, Lauren braced herself.

Garrett raised an eyebrow. "No problem. I'll just help the girls put the glasses and popcorn bowls away."

When the others had left the room, Gracie hobbled a few steps and Lauren met her the rest of the way.

"I just wanted to say, um, w-well…" she stammered, staring at the floor. "I've been a nasty ol' thing since I arrived here. Especially to you."

Had Lauren heard her right? Lauren took a teensy step closer.

"It's obvious how Garrett feels about you, and… well, I was jealous." She paused. "But when the brakes went out on that bike and I had no control on the highway…" Tears rolled down her cheeks. "I did some thinking at the hospital, and I've decided as much as I want a man to share my life with—" she looked up, gave a tiny chuckle and brushed the tear from her face "—I don't need one so badly that I hurt everyone around me." She hesitated. "I'm sorry, Lauren."

Lauren felt her own eyes start to sting. She reached over and hugged Gracie, taking care not to topple her.

Garrett entered the room.

"Well, good night," Gracie said, wiping her eyes.

"Good night, Gracie." Lauren turned to Garrett. "Good night," she said, then headed for her room. Her emotions swirled in confusion. Lauren wanted to dislike Gracie for what seemed to be developing between her and Garrett and for her past comments. Still, there was no denying the obvious change in her.

"Gracie, let me put my arm around you here, and you just sort of hop up the step with me."

Garrett's comment left Lauren with a sinking feeling in her stomach. Why had she allowed herself to fall in love again? She deserved the heartache for being so stupid. She stepped into her room and closed the door behind her, hoping to shut out the tenderness she could hear in Garrett's voice, the sweetness in Gracie's. Lauren just wanted to go somewhere far away from everyone she knew, a place where she could start over, where no one knew what a failure she was in work and in love.

Garrett grimaced when he pulled himself out of bed the next morning. He was stiff and sore. He hadn't slept well. Each movement through the night had brought aches and pains, but at least he was still alive and kicking. Well, alive anyway.

Truth be known, it was more than the pain that had bothered him. He knew he had to make a change in his life. He and God weren't exactly strangers, after all, and Garrett knew there would be no peace until he made some changes. And he knew just the person who could help him. Paul Burke.

Though it took some time, he showered, shaved and

got dressed. Afterward, he walked over to the phone in his room and called the church.

"Pastor Burke speaking."

"Paul, just the man I wanted to talk to."

"Garrett?"

The disbelief in the pastor's voice amused Garrett. He couldn't blame his friend really. Garrett didn't call him for three years, then all of a sudden he had lunch with him, then called two days later.

"Yeah, it's me. Sorry to be a pest, but I wondered if you had any openings in your schedule so I could pop in for a short talk?" Garrett's hands felt clammy just thinking about it.

"Sure do. In fact, now would be a good time, if you could manage it."

Garrett gulped. He figured God was giving him no time to back out.

"I'll be there in ten minutes."

"See you then."

"Sorry we've had to put off our date the past two nights, Billie," Garrett said as he walked her to the car.

"Like you had a choice. Don't worry about it. I'm surprised you can walk after that fiasco with you and Gracie on your bikes."

He let her in, then walked to his side and got in the car. "I admit I'm still a little sore. But also very hungry." He started the engine.

On the way to the restaurant Garrett pointed out some of the sights in the area. At the risk of being recognized, Garrett boldly revisited the steak house to which he had taken Nikki. He still wanted that steak, and since Nikki hadn't been the right person to eat the steak in front of, he wanted to go back. Besides, he knew Billie would not only allow him to enjoy the tender cut of beef, he would probably have to keep her fork out of his plate.

He loved the smell of grilled steak and spices, and lifted his nose appreciatively after the server took their orders and walked away.

"It does smell good in here," Billie said when she saw him. She rubbed her hands together. "Nothing as good as a thick hunk of beef."

He nodded, though with a little caution. She wasn't exactly the most soft-spoken woman he had ever met.

"You sure wouldn't want to bring Nikki to this place." She guffawed at her own joke.

Garrett swallowed hard. Okay, so he wasn't the brightest fish in the tank. He took a drink from the glass the server placed in front of him.

He sat back in his chair. "So tell me about yourself, Billie."

"What's to tell? I work at a fitness center. I hunt elk. I have five brothers, no sisters, which should tell you a lot." She gave a quick snort.

Garrett tried not to stare.

"I enjoy my life—I really do. I love Montana, the nature thing, the whole bit." She took a drink from her iced tea. "I know I'm not the same as other women my age. I'm into fitness because I enjoy the challenge of a workout, not because I want to keep skinny."

He suddenly felt weak and scrawny.

"Let's see, nothing I enjoy more than hunting elk. There's something about a fresh kill."

Okay, that frightened him a little.

She took another drink and grinned. For a moment he noticed the twinkle in her blue eyes. She really wasn't bad to look at, but he wouldn't want to cross her. She'd have him pinned to the floor before he knew what had hit him. The very idea made his already sore body shudder.

They talked a while longer about the Montana wilderness, hunting and fishing and how Montana compared to the Lake Tahoe area.

The server delivered their entrées.

Garrett wanted to sit there and hold the tender beef up to his nose. He cut a bite-sized chunk, lifted it to his mouth and hesitated. The image of a happy cow flashed upon the meat.

He ate it anyway.

The next morning Gracie and Ellen sat on the sofa in the great room, lost in their novels. Billie had gone for another bike ride, Nikki was shopping and Garrett had taken Macy to pick up some items she would need for her dorm room in the fall. Lauren sat in the great room with the others, browsing through a magazine. Molly entered the room.

"Um, Lauren?" She bit her lip.

Lauren looked up. "Yeah, Molly?"

"Well, there's, um, someone here to see you?"

"Someone is here to see *me?*" She couldn't imagine who, but then she wondered if Candace had decided to come for a visit. The possibility excited Lauren.

Before she could get up, footsteps sounded near the entrance and Lauren followed Molly's gaze.

"Hi, Lauren. Got a minute so we can talk?"

Lauren froze. She couldn't believe she was looking into the face of the very person who had broken her heart only six months ago.

"Hi, Jeff."

Everyone looked at him. Blond hair hung lazily across his forehead and stopped short of warm blue eyes. Dressed in stylish jeans and a nice crisp shirt, he still looked good—Lauren couldn't deny it. He flashed his straight white teeth. His smile could soften the hardest of hearts, though Lauren would never allow it to penetrate hers again.

At least, that was the plan.

Lauren made the necessary introductions, trying to keep her emotions in check. She didn't know how she felt right now—first with Garrett and Gracie, and now with Jeff showing up. She wanted to protect herself from more hurt.

"What are you doing here?" Lauren made no effort to move from her chair.

The confident, proud, Mr. I-can-conquer-the-world stuffed his hand in his pocket and fidgeted with what sounded like his keys. "Um, I thought maybe we could go to lunch?"

Lauren stared at him a moment. Was this the Jeff she knew? She had never once seen him appear nervous about anything. Until now.

"You came all the way here to take me to lunch?" She made no effort to welcome him and part of her felt ashamed about that, but another part tried to protect her.

"Not exactly." He looked at the others, then back to Lauren. "I was hoping we could talk."

She wanted to give him what for, right in front of

everyone, but she knew that would solve nothing. "Well, I guess it's all right." She looked around the room, noticing everyone was still watching the exchange. It might have been funny if she had not been so shocked by his presence. "Let me just go up to my room and get my bag."

Lauren's heart pounded harder than her footsteps as she climbed the stairs to her room. She grabbed her bag, applied a little more lipstick, ran a comb through her hair, then headed down the stairs with a prayer for wisdom in her heart.

Jeff opened the door for her, and once they stepped outside, he pointed toward his car. The expensive kind, with fancy wheels. Something new since he'd dumped her. With no honeymoon to pay for, he had money for a new car.

He pulled open the door for her. "You look great," he said, his face inches from hers.

She ducked her head and got inside.

"Where's a good place to eat?" he asked as he slipped into traffic.

Trying to ignore the familiar smell of his cologne, Lauren gave him directions to a nice Italian restaurant down the road. They pulled into a parking spot and he shut off the engine. His presence unnerved her beyond belief, and she just wanted to get this whole ordeal over with.

Garlic and pasta perfumed the air of the restaurant. The hostess seated Lauren and Jeff and the server took their orders before Jeff turned his attention to Lauren.

His blue eyes held hers. "I've missed you, Lauren—"

"What are you doing here, Jeff?" She cut him off in a none-too-friendly tone.

His eyebrows rose. "So that's how it is?"

"That's how it is."

"Won't you hear me out?"

"Look, you didn't travel all this way, six months after the fact, to explain your position, did you?"

He stared at her.

Though her heart stirred like a wild animal caged within the confines of her chest, she didn't so much as twitch. She would not let him break her resolve. Not this time.

He sighed and sat back against the booth. "I saw the little blurb on the news about you being here. The reporter mentioned your ex-fiancé. Me." He grinned. "Made me sound like a real jerk, by the way."

Okay, that made her feel better.

"At first I was mad. I wanted to come here and give you a piece of my mind. But when the camera gave the close-up of you, I couldn't deny how it made me feel." He leaned into the table. "I realized how badly I had screwed up my life." He thought a moment. "Listen, Lauren, Camilla and I were over a week after you left the office. You would have known that if you had let me talk to you at the office or if you had answered my calls."

She had heard the office gossip. "So is that supposed to make a difference to me, Jeff? The fact that you and Camilla are over?"

He reached for her hand, but she shrank back.

He stopped abruptly. "I thought it might."

"It doesn't. You think you can come over here just because you've tired of Camilla and waltz back into my life?"

The server brought their drinks. Lauren took a deep

breath and settled back in her seat while the server placed the glasses in front of them.

"Listen, I got scared, okay? Do you have any idea what emotions can do to a person?"

Murder came to mind, but she kept silent.

"I know, it sounds pathetic even to me. But that's the way it was."

Lauren measured her words. "It's been six months, Jeff. Why are you just now coming to me?"

"You wouldn't talk to me at the office. You ignored my phone calls. I sent e-mails you never answered and most likely didn't read. I didn't know how to get in touch with you. Until the news clip. I thought after all this time—"

"It's too late for all that now, Jeff."

"I thought you loved me."

"I thought you loved me, too."

Jeff raked his hand through his hair. "You're not making this easy."

"I'm not making this easy? Do you have any idea what you and Camilla put me through while you worked through your little wedding-jitters crisis? You betrayed me—with my *best friend!*" She could feel her cheeks flame.

His sad eyes met hers. "I can only imagine, and I'm sorry."

"You're sorry."

"What else can I say, Lauren?"

"There is nothing to say, Jeff. It's over."

Silence stretched between them, allowing her the time she needed to calm down. "Believe it or not, Jeff, I have forgiven you and Camilla. I mean, it hurt. A lot. But we all make mistakes, and I do forgive you."

He brightened.

"But there is no future for us. I didn't see that before, but you actually did us both a favor. We had been together forever. We had a comfortable relationship. It seemed natural we would get married one day." Lauren fidgeted with a napkin on the table. "But it's right that we've moved on with our lives."

He sat silent for a while. Finally he said, "There is something else."

As the server placed their meals of spaghetti and meatballs, garlic bread and salad on the table, Lauren didn't want to begin to think what his "something else" might be.

Maybe she'd choke on a meatball and would never have to find out.

A tune came over his cell phone. Lauren thought "Your Cheating Heart" would be a good tune for him.

"Will you excuse me?" he said, grabbing his phone and leaving the table before Lauren could answer him.

Okay, instead of choking on a meatball, a phone call would work.

"Macy, since we have a few places yet to go, would you mind if we stopped for some coffee?" Garrett pulled the car to a stop at the red light.

"What's the matter, am I wearing you out already?"

"A little caffeine couldn't hurt." He winked. Pushing on the accelerator, he headed toward the coffee shop and a much-needed break. Though Garrett teased his daughter, he had more important things in mind than caffeine. He had some repair work to do.

They got their coffees and sat down at a table. Macy

scratched off her list the items she had purchased that morning. She looked over the remaining list. "Doesn't look too bad. We should be finished in another hour—maybe less."

Garrett looked at his watch. "Really? That should put us close to lunch. Want to go somewhere after we're finished shopping?"

"You sure you want to?"

"And why wouldn't I want to take my beautiful daughter around town?"

"Okay, what's up?"

"What do you mean?"

"Look, Dad, we've not exactly been getting along real great for the past, oh, I don't know, three years—in case you haven't noticed."

"I've noticed. Hey, how about we drive down to the park?"

She stared at him.

"Come on, Macy. It's a nice day."

"But it's more than that, isn't it, Dad?"

"We need to talk."

They both picked up their coffee cups and headed through the doors, to what Garrett hoped would be a better future.

Chapter Nineteen

"Sorry about the interruption," Jeff said as he slid into his side of the booth.

Lauren looked at him and then down at her cold spaghetti. Par for the course.

He started to dig in to his meal. No longer intimidated by him, Lauren bowed her head and prayed. He used to tell her it bothered him that she did that in public, drew attention to herself. His comment had made her feel as though she was doing it for show. She knew, of course, that wasn't true, but he'd made her feel that way. It was his way of manipulating her to do what he wanted.

Not this time.

When she finished and picked up her fork, she could feel him looking at her, but she ignored him. "So you were about to tell me something." She speared a meatball and put it in her mouth.

"Um, yeah. Well, as I was saying—well, I guess I wasn't actually saying it, but I was getting to it, but what I meant to say was..."

It was all Lauren could do to keep the meatball from falling out of her mouth. What in the world was he babbling on about? No, wait. Mr. I'm-having-a-good-hair-day-and-I'm-in-control was babbling? Oh, this was good. Lauren shifted into a comfortable position in the booth, leaned back and savored the moment, the meatball, everything.

Life was good.

He saw her response. A hard edge crept into his face. "Okay, Lauren, it's like this. The firm wants you back. We need you. We've got a couple of clients who are refusing to do business with us if you don't handle their cases."

Oh, this day couldn't get any better.

She sat up straighter and casually took a mouthful of spaghetti. Why rush this whole lunch thing?

Jeff practically gaped at her.

"You'd better eat your spaghetti before it gets cold." Oh, she was enjoying herself. She knew Jeff was dying to continue this conversation, but why the big hurry? She slowed her chewing. A few more bites of spaghetti and garlic bread, then she looked at him. How curious. His face had turned a lovely shade of red. Crimson, really. No, more like a burgundy color. No, no, definitely brighter than that. Now that she thought about it, the shade was more of the orange-red family, kind of like what you would find at the tip of a hot iron.

"Lauren?"

She could almost see smoke coming from his ears. "Which clients?" Feigning innocence, she sort of batted her eyelashes. She had learned a few things from Gracie.

"Two big ones. I think you know," he barked.

"Let's see, Lighting the Way Corporation and..." She covered her mouth with her left fist and looked toward the ceiling.

"It's..."

She held up her right palm and squeezed her eyes shut. "No, no. Don't tell me! It's right on the tip of my tongue." She thought some more. "Um, the Hathaways," she said with exaggerated enthusiasm, thinking of the wealthy family who had practically made her one of their own.

Jeff sneered.

She clapped her hands. "I knew it!"

"So what's your price?"

"What?"

"Boss man says get you to name your price."

"Wait a minute. Is this why you came to find me? All that garbage about wanting me back..." She stopped when she saw the look on his face. His expression told her everything.

Her eyes narrowed. "Why did they send you to discuss something so personal with me? Did the partners think you might have extra pull or something?"

Jeff kept silent.

"Unbelievable! Your dad, of all people, should have known they would have a better chance if he or one of the partners had approached me." She thought a moment. "Look, Jeff, you tell your dad—or whoever—if they want me to come back, they'll have to call and discuss the matter with me themselves. You're not involved in my personal affairs. We're not engaged anymore, remember?"

His eyebrows rose. "Suit yourself."

* * *

Garrett watched Macy's face as he poured out his heart to her, revealing his step of faith earlier in the pastor's office, how he was relying on God to help him meet each new day, one breath at a time. He told her he'd finally realized he had become a recluse, just as she had said, pretty much hiding out in the B and B. He wanted to live again.

"Now comes the hard part." He reached for her hand. Her eyes were wide and unblinking. "I need to ask for your forgiveness for Mom's death."

Macy gasped.

"I know it was all my fault, Macy. I wish I could change things, but I can't." Tears swelled in his eyes, making it hard to see her. "She asked me to get that tire fixed, and I put it off. When I finally got around to getting the car into the repair shop, it was too late." He pulled his hand from hers and swiped the tears from his face. "I killed her just as sure as we're sitting here."

Macy grabbed his arm. "No, Dad! Stop!"

"But, Macy—"

"No! Don't you see? You didn't do it. I did!" She was crying now.

Her words hit him like a blow to the face.

"I thought you knew Mom and I had an argument before she went out that day. She was upset. I thought you blamed me. I—"

He reached for her. "Oh, no, baby, you didn't do it."

"I did." She covered her face with her hands and sobbed.

Garrett got up from his side of the picnic table and pulled her into a warm embrace. "I bought an outfit she didn't approve of," Macy said between sobs. "She told me I had to return it." A hiccup and more sobs. "We had words. She took the outfit from me and said she was returning it right then and there." Macy cried some more. She looked up at Garrett, pain all over her face. "I yelled after her, Dad. She stormed out of the house. I never saw Mom alive again." She covered her face again, and her body heaved with great sobs. With tears streaming down his own face, Garrett pulled his daughter tighter against him, praying God would give him the strength to help her through this.

There in the quiet of the park, with only a couple of wandering passersby, Garrett and Macy cried away three years of grief and misunderstandings. When their emotions were finally spent, Garrett leaned away from Macy.

"You gonna be okay?"

With swollen eyes she looked up at him and sniffed. "Yeah." She blotted her face with the handkerchief he had given her.

They sat in silence a little longer while he held her as a father trying to protect his child. "We're gonna make it, Mace."

She looked up at him and gave a weak smile. "Yeah, Dad, I think you're right."

Garrett gave her one more squeeze for good measure. "You ready to go finish that shopping and have some lunch?"

She nodded.

Macy settled upon a comforter for her dorm bed sooner than Garrett had anticipated. He carried the package and they made their way to the car.

"I don't know about you, but all that crying made me hungry."

Macy laughed. A sound he hadn't heard in so long, he wanted to linger in it.

"Thanks for letting me get some more makeup, Dad." Macy pulled down the visor, looked into the mirror and touched up her eyes and lips.

"No problem, honey." They decided on a place to eat and drove up to the restaurant.

"You know, I'm getting pretty hungry myself," Macy said once Garrett shut off the engine.

"Great. Let's go."

They entered the eatery and talked about their purchases while they waited for the hostess to seat them.

"Come this way," the woman said.

Garrett allowed Macy to go first and he followed. Just as they were about to be seated, he came face-to-face with Lauren and some man.

"Garrett. Macy. Um, hi."

Garrett looked from Lauren to the man and back to Lauren.

"Garrett and Macy, this is Jeff Levinger."

Jeff Levinger. As in former fiancé. Garrett swallowed hard.

"Jeff, this is the man who owns the bed-and-breakfast where I'm staying, and this is his daughter."

Jeff's eyebrows rose. "The man looking for a woman," he said, making no attempt to hide his amusement. As if Garrett couldn't get a woman any other way.

Garrett wanted to deck him, but he took a deep breath instead.

"Jeff is here on business."

Garrett eyed her suspiciously. He knew Lauren wouldn't lie, but something in the way she said it made him think there was more to it. He could easily imagine what.

Jeff grinned.

Garrett gritted his teeth.

"Well, I'll see you back at the house," Lauren said.

Garrett knew they had no ties between them, but he also knew he had fallen in love with Lauren. It seemed ridiculous when he thought of how long they had known each other. Still, he hoped they could get to know one another better and see where it might lead them. With her ex-fiancé showing up, Garrett figured he had little chance with her now.

"You haven't said much," Macy said as she and Garrett sat at the table.

Garrett shoved the spaghetti around on his plate. "Yeah, I know."

"Listen, Dad, I know it looks bad, but I think you should talk to Lauren."

"Yeah, maybe you're right," he said softly, still staring at his plate.

The more he thought about it, the more he thought Macy was right. He should talk to Lauren. And he would. As soon as he had the chance.

When Lauren got back to the B and B, she had decided to go shopping. That usually made her feel better. But not this time. She could hardly think straight. How many stores had she trudged through already this afternoon? And still her mind was muddled.

Jeff's presence had unnerved her, to say the least, but she had gotten through it much better than she would ever have imagined. It also confirmed to her that she had never loved him in the true sense of the word. Cared for him like a comfortable old shoe, yes. Loved him as a woman should love the man she marries, no.

Then the whole thing about work—well, that had certainly taken her by surprise.

"May I help you, ma'am?" a salesclerk wanted to know.

"Oh, thank you, no. I'm just looking."

"If you need any assistance, please let me know." The woman headed for the next customer.

Lauren ran her fingers along the sleek black leather boots with the trendy heels. They were nice. She looked at the sticker price. If she had a job, she probably wouldn't hesitate to buy them.

It felt good to be needed, appreciated. That was the painful part of losing her job. It had made her feel she had no value or self-worth. Still, was this what she wanted to do for the rest of her life?

Her cell phone sounded. She stepped away from the aisle and dug through her handbag. "Hello?"

"Hi, it's Candace. How are things going?"

Lauren sighed and edged toward a secluded spot to talk. "Oh, Candace, I'm so glad you called. I have no idea what I'm going to do."

"Really? What's up?"

Lauren explained Jeff's visit, the job opportunity, Gracie and Garrett's near accident and the change in them both.

Candace whistled. "And to think I thought you had no cares in the world while you were there."

"What am I going to do, Candace?"

"Do you love him?"

"Who?"

"Garrett Cantrell, that's who."

Lauren thought a moment, almost afraid to say the word. "Yes," she finally said in a near whisper.

"I thought so."

"How is it possible, Candace? I mean, I hardly know him."

"Well, look at you and Jeff. You've known him for years and you thought you loved him."

"Goes to show you I can't trust myself."

"No, it shows that just because you've dated someone for a long time doesn't mean you love him."

"I don't know."

"Look, Lauren, no one is telling you to get married next week. I'm just saying give your feelings a chance. This guy may be the one, and you don't want to pass him up."

"Didn't you hear anything I said about Gracie and Garrett?"

"I heard."

"And?"

"And what? There is nothing in what you've said that makes me think his feelings have changed about you."

"But his feelings for her have changed."

"Okay, so he thinks she's nice now instead of a spoiled brat. Still doesn't mean he's switched his love from you to her. It doesn't work that way."

"And what has made you so smart, Miss Marriage Counselor Woman?" Lauren teased.

"You know, always the bridesmaid, never the bride. I've learned from watching my friends."

"The thing I'm most concerned about is I don't know where Garrett stands in his relationship with God. I mean, he's made little hints that he's working back toward the relationship they used to share, but he's not there yet. I'm not about to get into another relationship where we can't share our faith."

"I understand. And you're right. That would not be good. You and God will have to work that one out. I'll pray that He'll give you direction, Lauren."

"Thanks."

"You know, you might have to leave there to think clearly. As long as Garrett is around, your emotions could get in the way."

Lauren hadn't thought of that. In fact, she didn't want to think about it. She dreaded Saturday already, but to leave early?

"Are you there?"

"Yeah, I'm here. You're probably right, Candace. I'll have to think about that one."

"Well, call me if you need me, okay?"

"Yeah. Thanks."

Lauren clicked off her phone. She had already wasted away the afternoon. A glance at her watch told her it was far later than she had realized. Seven o'clock. No wonder her stomach was growling. She had no idea she had wandered around for so long. She'd get back to the bed-and-breakfast. Maybe she could find some answers there.

Lauren mentally went over what she had to do once she returned to the B and B. Fortunately, Molly had agreed to care for Nocchi while Lauren was gone. Though Lauren might need to take her dog out when she got there.

She pulled her rental car up to the B and B parking lot. Thursday night already. Tomorrow she hoped to check out any last-minute places she had failed to visit yet. First thing Saturday morning she was up and out the door to catch her flight. The very idea made her moody. With a sigh she grabbed her keys, dumped them into her handbag and headed for the front door.

Her mind still occupied with the day's events, she stepped inside. There in the hallway stood Gracie and Garrett in an embrace. Lauren stood transfixed for a moment, totally unable to think, move or speak. Seems she always showed up at the wrong time.

Garrett stepped away from Gracie. "Lauren, we've been wondering where you were."

"Hi, Lauren," Gracie said with no hint of victory in her face.

Lauren smiled at Gracie, then cleared her throat. "Well, it's been a long day," she said, offering no explanation about her day.

"I'm sure it has," Garrett said.

"Um, good night," Lauren said, edging her way past them. She heard them go out the door as she trudged up the stairs. Well, it looked as though God had given her His answer. No use prolonging the agony.

She'd try to get a flight out tomorrow.

Chapter Twenty

Refusing to fall into a puddle of tears, Lauren set to work packing her suitcase. The sooner she could leave this place the better. A tear or two slipped down her cheek. Okay, so maybe she would cry just a little.

Pulling her clean shorts from the drawer, she folded them and put them in the suitcase. She was thankful the girls had allowed her to use the washer and dryer so she could take clean clothes home. That would free her up once she got back to Indiana.

What had made her think any of this would work? As if her life wasn't bad enough before she made this trip, here she was two weeks later, in love with someone else entirely, with no hope of romance.

"You're an idiot, Lauren Romey, that's what." She stomped across the floor, yanked open a drawer, pulled out her shirts, went back to the suitcase and threw them inside. She didn't care that her suitcase was a mess. Airport security usually rummaged through it anyway, destroying whatever semblance of order she might have managed.

That reminded her. She had to call the airport and see about getting her flight changed or she could be stuck there all day tomorrow. The last thing she needed was to stick around and watch Garrett and Gracie plan their wedding.

The thought caused her to stuff her remaining possessions into the now bulging suitcase. She probably shouldn't have made those extra purchases. Too late now.

With that task finished, she picked up the phone and dialed the eight hundred number for the airlines. Once she talked to the airline personnel and made the necessary arrangements, she hung up the phone. Her flight would leave at ten o'clock the next morning. She'd leave the B and B around eight. That would give her time to say goodbye, but hopefully leave before she had to see Garrett and Gracie together at breakfast."

Planning to just get up and go in the morning, Lauren quickly showered and prepared for bed. The house was quiet. She wondered if Garrett and Gracie were back yet. Without further thought, she walked over to the window and peeked out. His car was back. Relief washed over her. Not that it mattered. So they were back. They were probably in the great room doing who knew what. She knew better than that, but still her emotions dictated her thoughts right now.

Placing her suitcase beside the door, she set her alarm and slipped into bed for her last night as Cinderella in the prince's castle. She winced. She was Cinderella, all right. And she was locked away in the tower with no hope for a happy-ever-after.

"Garrett, I had a great time tonight," Gracie said in the car as they made their way back to the bed-and-breakfast. "I'm sorry about that little incident in front of Lauren. Do you want me to talk to her?"

"No, thanks, Gracie. I doubt that it matters one way or another. I told you about her fiancé. I'm sure she'll head back to him." He turned to her. "By the way, you sure seem different these days."

"Well, I can't deny that that bike ride changed me. I doubt that I will ever be the same again."

"I know exactly what you mean."

"You, too?"

"Uh-hum." He explained about his time with the pastor. "I figure if God hasn't given up on me, anyone has a chance."

Gracie looked at him. "That's good to know."

"You've been a good friend, Gracie. I'll be praying for you in the days ahead that the Lord will bring just the right person into your life."

"You know, somehow I think He will. When He's ready, and when I'm ready."

"We have changed, haven't we?"

She nodded.

"I think I'll have a talk with Lauren tomorrow. See just where she stands with Jeff and where she stands with me."

"I think that's a good idea, Garrett. I know a little bit about women, and…well, that woman is in love with you. It's all over her face."

"I hope you're right."

"I'm right. You'll see."

Someone had been in the kitchen. The muffins were on a tray. Lauren could smell some kind of sausage breakfast casserole baking in the oven. Hopefully, she would see at least Garrett and the girls to say goodbye.

When Lauren stepped into the dining room, Garrett stood facing her.

"You're leaving?" The shadows beneath his eyes stood in contrast to his pale skin. Lauren wondered if he was coming down with something.

She tried to sound cheerful. "Yeah, I got an early flight out. Figured I needed to get back. Um, Jeff mentioned the senior partners want me to return to work for them." She mustered a bright smile.

Garrett studied her. She wished he wouldn't do that. "Is that what you want?"

His question jarred her for just a moment. "What? Oh, yeah, sure. I mean, there are bills to pay and all." She smiled again.

Macy and Molly joined them.

"You're leaving already?" Macy's sad eyes almost made Lauren lose her resolve. She swallowed hard.

"We wish you didn't have to go so soon," Molly added.

"She can't stay here forever, girls. She has a life back in Indiana." Garrett's gaze stayed locked with hers. "We wish you the best, Lauren."

Her heart flipped while tears threatened.

"Good morning, Lauren," Gracie said, walking into view, with the other contestants right behind her.

Lauren pulled herself together long enough to hug everyone goodbye. Afterwards, Macy, Molly and the contestants wandered into the dining area. Garrett stayed behind. The last one to hug her goodbye. As he held her close, his warm breath brushed against her ear.

"I wish—"

"Sorry to interrupt you, Dad, but you have a phone call," Molly said.

Garrett sighed, pulled back and looked Lauren straight in the eyes. "Take care, Lauren."

He walked away.

Lauren bent over to pick up her things.

"I have to talk to you."

Lauren looked up to see Macy standing there.

"I know you're in a hurry, but I have to let you know what happened."

Macy told Lauren about her dad's appointment with the pastor, the way Garrett had explained it to her. Then she told Lauren how Garrett had taken her to the park and there they had talked out their grief over her mother's death.

Lauren warmed to the information. "Oh, Macy, I'm so happy for you both. I've been praying for you." She choked back the tears.

"Dad loves you, Lauren."

"Macy, please don't make this any harder than it is. I have to go. Keep in touch, okay." Her heart ached for this teenager, but Lauren couldn't allow Macy's wants to overshadow the truth.

Tears pooled in Macy's eyes as they hugged and said goodbye once more. Lauren kept telling herself not to cry as she grabbed her handbag, suitcase, and Nocchi's cage and headed for her rental car. She'd been through a broken heart before—she could get through it again.

Before she could grow too somber, she slipped out the back door, let Nocchi take care of business and say goodbye to Bear. "Goodbye ol' boy," Lauren said, scratching Garrett's dog behind his right ear. She was even going to miss the dog. Good grief, she needed a life. "Okay, doggies, time is up. Have a good life, Bear." Lauren scooped Nocchi into her arms, took her over to the carrier and put her in. Once inside the car, Lauren strapped the carrier in, then she pulled on her own seat belt. "Ready, girl?" She started the car and drove to the airport.

On the way there, she decided she'd use the weekend to rest, then she'd call her old office on Monday morning to see how serious they were about rehiring her. She would probably accept. Though the idea of working someplace else, starting all over again, was enticing, she had to face reality. And the reality was she had bills to pay.

Her thoughts drifted to Garrett and Macy. She hoped they could work things out between them before Macy went off to college. Lauren prayed for them. Maybe Macy would write and let her know how things were going. She'd no doubt hear of Gracie and Garrett's wedding announcement one day. That she could do without.

Nocchi whimpered in the seat beside her.

"I know, girl. We'll be home soon."

Home. Usually that thought made her feel better. But not this time. Her heart now belonged somewhere else.

* * *

Macy walked into Garrett's den just as he got off the phone.

"You doing okay?" she asked.

"I'm fine, why?" He straightened some papers on his desk, not wanting his daughter to see the pain he was feeling.

"With Lauren leaving early and all."

"She's made her choice, Macy, and that's that." He slapped his legs as he pushed himself up from the chair.

"I don't believe you."

He whirled around. "What do you want me to do, Macy—grovel? The woman has made her decision."

"You have no idea what made her go home. Maybe it's because she saw you and Gracie hugging when she got home last night."

"How do you know about that?"

"Gracie told me. She feels responsible for it all."

"Well, that's just ridiculous. I'm sure it had nothing to do with that."

"You have no idea what it has to do with. That's what I'm saying, Dad—you need to go after her. Let her know how you feel. Let her know that you have made peace with God. Let her know you can't live without her."

"Who said I can't live without her?"

"Dad, please. Everyone knows."

He rubbed the back of his neck. "I'm that obvious?"

She raised her eyebrows. "Uh-huh."

Just then Molly entered the room. She placed balled fists firmly on her hips, her gaze going from her dad to Macy, and back to her dad. "Well?"

"Well, what?" Garrett asked, trying to shake the image of Molly as some kind of superhero.

"Are you going?"

"Going where?"

"To the airport," Molly and Macy said in unison.

Garrett thought this whole episode was looking suspiciously like a conspiracy to get him and Lauren together.

"You'd better get there before you lose her to Romeo," Molly said.

"I just hope you haven't wasted too much time already," Macy added.

Both girls were already leading him to the door.

"Wait a minute. Hold everything," he said, trying to reclaim his familial position. "I'm the dad here."

The girls nodded and continued to nudge him toward the door.

"I decide what's best for our family."

More smiles and nods.

"I determine what course to take next."

Giggles and nods.

"And I choose—"

"To go to the airport," the girls said together pointing toward the door.

"I get no respect around here," he grumbled as he grabbed his keys and headed out the door.

Lauren wandered aimlessly through the crowd at the airport, going through the usual routine of checking in.

Emotionally, she felt like she had been up all day by the time she settled into her seat. She turned her wrist to check the time but she wasn't wearing her watch.

Thinking a moment, it hit her. She had taken her watch off to shower and left it on the sink. Her parents had given her that watch for her last birthday, so she had to get it back. Maybe Garrett would send it to her. Was that too much to ask? They had been so kind to her already.

At her gate, a voice called over the loud speaker, notifying the passengers that their flight was canceled. *Great. Just great.* Everyone scrambled to get in line to book a new one.

Lauren could have gotten a connecting flight late that evening, but she didn't like traveling alone so late at night and decided to opt for the first available flight the next day. Her funds were dwindling quickly, so she hoped she could find a reasonable hotel near the airport.

With the arrangements made, she picked up her luggage and dog carrier, then headed out of the airport. Now that she was no longer in a hurry, she decided she'd grab a bit of breakfast and then head back to the B and B to get her watch. No sense in leaving Garrett with the expense of returning it. If she ran into Garrett and Gracie, so be it.

Garrett couldn't deny the definite charge in his adrenaline when he learned that Lauren's flight had been canceled. He wasn't sure why, though. It wasn't likely he would find her in the airport. She could have found another flight. Even if she didn't, he doubted that she would come back to the B and B to stay the night.

He glanced at one person, then the next, hoping to find her in the throng of people milling through the airport. He had a feeling she would be here a while.

* * *

Lauren wasn't sure if she was relieved or disappointed when the taxi pulled up to the B and B and she saw that Garrett's and the girls' cars were gone. Evidently, the girls had taken the contestants out again. Maybe Garrett went along.

She walked up to the door, but it was locked. Once again she grabbed her suitcase and Nocchi's carrier, and trudged to the back of the B and B. When she spotted Bear, she set her luggage down and pulled Nocchi from her carrier. Together, they went over to visit Bear who was now standing with tail wagging.

"Well, you're a welcome sight, ol' boy." She scratched his ears. "I sure wish you could tell me where everyone is." Lauren petted the dog a while longer, then straightened and stretched her legs. Since she had the time and no one was here, she decided to take one last walk into the woods.

Without the weight of the luggage, Lauren felt a little relief from the tension that had plagued her all morning. The cool of the forest whispered across her skin, making it tingle as she stepped into the shade. She walked over to the bench that had become her favorite spot as well as Garrett's and sat down. Whether from the day's tension, being in this place or thinking of Garrett, she didn't know, but she quickly erupted into a puddle of tears.

She buried her face in her hands. "Oh, God, what am I going to do? I love him. We finally work out all our differences—well, most of them anyway—and he falls in love with someone else. What am I going to do? Garrett is in love with someone else."

"Well, I don't know where you get your information, but you'd better recheck your sources."

Lauren's head shot up. "Garrett!"

He broke into a wide grin and sat down beside her.

She sniffed. "What did you hear?"

He pulled a handkerchief from his back pocket. "Everything." Tenderly he reached up and blotted a tear from her face, then another, then another.

"But I—"

"Shh." He pressed his finger against her lips. "You've told me all that I need to know, Lauren Romey." His finger trailed across her lips and traced the side of her cheek. "I love you, Lauren. I've loved you from the first day I set eyes on you." His finger continued up the side of her cheek and tucked her hair behind her ear as his mouth descended to hers, claiming her softly, like the brush of the wind upon her lips. "I love you, Lauren Romey." His lips played upon her own, his breath mingling with hers, neither daring to pull away.

Lauren thought she had stepped into a dream where suddenly all was right with her world.

He pulled her to him. "I never thought I could love again, but you've changed all that. Don't ever leave me, Lauren." He held her close for a long moment. He finally looked at her. "You're probably concerned that we haven't known each other long, but I'm willing to wait for you however long it takes to make you my wife."

Lauren could hardly snap out of her dreamy fog.

"Did you hear me, Lauren? I'm asking you to marry me."

She looked at him. "Yes! Yes! A thousand times, yes!"

They embraced once more. Sitting in the silence, Lauren suddenly realized they had a lot of questions to answer.

"What about Gracie?"

"A friend."

"Nothing more?"

"Nothing. What about Jeff?"

"A person in my past."

"Not your future?"

She shook her head.

He smiled.

"What will I do for a job while we plan our wedding?"

"I have an attorney friend who's looking for a temporary attorney to help with his caseload. Needs someone for about four months. His current partner is on bed rest for maternity leave. I know you want something more permanent—"

"I'd have to pass the bar exam to practice here, but it sounds perfect."

"It does?"

"Yes! Once we're married, maybe I could go practice law part-time and help you at the B and B, if you don't mind?"

Wide-eyed, he stared at her, then threw his head back and laughed. "God is amazing! That's exactly what I had hoped for." He squeezed her tight again. "Wait a minute. What about you still having to live in a small town—can you handle that?"

"As long as you take me to the big city every now and then."

"You got it."

"A little traveling during the slow season?"

He nodded.

"I get to keep my laptop."

He grinned. "Check."

"Pocket PC?"

"Check."

"Get to go to the spa now and then, have my nails done—"

"Yes, yes, a thousand times, yes!"

She laughed. "All right, here's the real test."

He searched her face.

"Nocchi still gets to wear her dresses and hats?"

Okay, he hesitated here. For a moment it looked as if things could go either way, but love finally won out. "If she must."

Lauren clapped and they kissed once more.

"By the way, I went to the airport and found out your flight was canceled—"

"You did?" The very idea that Garrett went to that trouble to find her thrilled her to no end.

He nodded. "I searched for you everywhere, then finally gave up and came home."

Lauren looked at him and smiled.

"So, what made you come back here?" he asked.

"My watch."

He looked confused. She laughed and explained to him about leaving her watch behind.

"Lucky for me you left it." He hugged her once more.

"Lauren, I know we have a few more things to settle and work through, but for now, how about we go in and tell the girls?"

"They're home?" Lauren couldn't contain her excitement.

"Macy spotted your luggage. They're probably watching for us right now out the back window." He laughed.

Lauren got up. Garrett grabbed her hand and intertwined it with his own. As they stepped into the clearing, the back door flew open. Macy and Molly ran out to them, and they all fell into each other's arms.

"I knew it would work out. I just knew it," Macy finally said.

"See, you were ready to adopt us out, but we came through for you. Somebody did Win Daddy's Heart," Molly added.

Garrett winked at the girls, then pulled Lauren next to him. "You're right, girls. You knew me better than I knew myself. And this gal—" he looked at Lauren "—did forever win my heart."

Underneath an afternoon sky Garrett pulled Lauren close to him once more and kissed her tenderly while Macy and Molly turned the other way and laughed. Then with a heart full of love and hope for bright tomorrows, the soon-to-be family made their way back to the bed-and-breakfast to plan for a wedding and a new life…together.

* * * * *

Dear Reader,

I hope you enjoyed reading this story. I had such fun visiting the Lake Tahoe area! I imagined my characters enjoying the view of snow-capped mountains on a moonlit night and feeling the brisk damp air brush against their faces as they took a cruise on the *Tahoe Queen.*

Lauren Romey and Garrett Cantrell encountered difficulties in their lives that made them wonder if they could ever trust anyone again. Still, both learned that while life can be uncertain, they could put their hands in the hand of the One who would get them through anything life could hurl their way.

When someone we care about lets us down, it's sometimes hard to trust that person again. Making ourselves vulnerable, exposing our hearts to possible pain, takes great courage. Sometimes it's worth the effort. Sometimes not. Still, in God's Word, *Proverbs* 3:5–6 "Trust in the Lord with all your heart and lean not on your own understanding; in all your ways acknowledge Him, and He will make your paths straight."

Does that mean everything will be perfect in our lives? No. We live in an imperfect world. But it does mean we are never alone. God walks with us every step of the way, through every joy, every pain, and He knows better than anyone what is best for us.

So, if you're struggling with trust, I hope you will consider the One who is trustworthy. Life is hard, but God is always good. Take a risk and trust Him. Your life will never be the same.

Diann